shadow
Breakers

shadow Breakers

BY DANIEL BLYTHE

Chicken House

SCHOLASTIC INC.
NEW YORK

All rights reserved. Published by Chicken House, an imprint of Scholastic Inc.,
Publishers since 1920. CHICKEN HOUSE, SCHOLASTIC,
and associated logos are trademarks and/or registered trademarks of Scholastic Inc.
www.scholastic.com

First published in the United Kingdom in 2012 as *Shadow Runners*
by Chicken House, 2 Palmer Street, Frome, Somerset BA11 1DS.
www.doublecluck.com

Library of Congress Cataloging-in-Publication Data

Blythe, Daniel.
Shadow breakers / by Daniel Blythe. — 1st American ed.
p. cm.
Summary: After moving from London to what seems like a dull seaside town,
twelve-year-old Miranda is recruited by a group of friends from school to help
identify and stop the evil that is shadowing Miranda and causing
weird events in town.
ISBN 978-0-545-47979-0
[1. Good and evil — Fiction. 2. Psychic ability — Fiction. 3. Supernatural —
Fiction. 4. Family life — England — Fiction. 5. Moving, Household — Fiction.
6. England — Fiction. 7. Mystery and detective stories.] I. Title.

PZ7.B6279Sh 2013
[Fic] — dc23

2012011273

10 9 8 7 6 5 4 3 2 1   13 14 15 16 17

Printed in the U.S.A.   23

First American edition, January 2013
The text type was set in Electra.
Book design by Natalie C. Sousa

FOR MY FAMILY

the 24-hour clock

CHAPTER ONE

dreamtime

EVERY NIGHT I TELL MYSELF THE DREAM WON'T come again. *Do not dream,* I recite like a mantra. *Do not dream.* But it's no use. It's been there ever since we moved from London three weeks ago, and sleep just creeps up my sheets the same as it always does, gobbling me up, swamping me. So I dream. And then, in the darkness, I see it.

The Shape.

It doesn't give me a shock or a jolt, like when you see a spider suddenly scuttle for cover. It's more a creeping chill, like you get from walking through a graveyard, or when you know someone hidden is watching you. We did a poem in school about a man who "walks a lonely road and dares not turn his head." How does it go on? Something about a frightful fiend treading close behind.

I call it the Shape because I don't know what it is. It's just . . . formless, like a shimmering, ever-changing shadow. But somehow I know — *I just know* — it's made of three things: fire and water and the purest, coldest darkness.

And then there's the whisper.

Miranda. Come away, Miranda. Come to me.

That's when I wake up, when I hear the whisper.

Okay, so you know the score. You've seen bad movies.

When people do "waking up from bad dreams" acting, they gasp, *uuuuuh!* and sit bolt upright. That *so* does not happen in real life. I'm always wrapped in my sheets, or lying at an odd angle across the bed. But I do sort of spasm, as if I'm falling from a great height. And then I untwist, and realize where I am — in this new house, this new place — and my eyes try to open, even though they feel glued together.

There's no hope of getting back to sleep, so I go downstairs and get a glass of water, trying not to wake Mum and Truffle. The running tap is a lonely sound as the sky turns from black to purple, the streetlamps grow dim, and the world wakes. And in the distance is the sound of the sea.

Not sleeping is becoming a problem.

I'd give anything not to dream.

* * *

My name is Miranda Keira May. I'm twelve, almost thirteen, and I live in Firecroft Bay. It's getting easier to say. We came here, Mum, me, and my baby brother, Truffle, after . . . well, after what happened. It was in the news. People know.

My brother's not really named Truffle, of course — his actual name is Thomas Patrick Zachary May. But as soon as he was born I called him Truffle, because when I first saw him he was wrapped in a fluffy towel, like a white chocolate truffle. It sort of stuck.

Oh, and the Patrick part comes from my dad, Patrick May.

2

Yep, *the* Patrick May, known as Paddy May, the man they called Mr. TV. The guy from *May I Present*, the biggest afternoon talk show on TV here in the UK. Only not anymore.

Yes, I miss him. Of course I do.

Every single day.

I think about how he used to take me swimming and to the playground and to the movies. How he'd smile and never get mad at me, and always call me Panda, his name for me since I was a toddler.

But now he's gone, and Mum's brought us to this dead-end place. Dullsville. The back of beyond, the middle of nowhere, the end of the world. A sad place, in both senses of the word, you know: as in a sad film, like *Bambi*, and the "you sad loser" sense. It's the kind of town where people go to die. Where the air smells of fish and seaweed, all splurging together into one seasidey, rotten smell. Where old men shuffle into seafront shelters in the cold, salty wind to eat melting ice-cream cones, and teenagers on bikes rattle up and down the Esplanade, giving them lip.

A chilly, prowling mist rolls in from the sea sometimes. It's so thick you can barely see where you're going, and it can last from a few hours to a few days. Mum says they called it *sea fret* where she grew up.

There isn't even any *sand* here. Just pebbles as far as you can see, from the harbor all the way to Whitecliff and the posh marina, where the chic apartments and expensive boats are. There's a halfhearted pier, which seems to be closed most of the time, and rows of pastel-colored motels and inns with cheerful names like "Sunrise" and "Bayview," though they've all got "VACANCIES" signs in their windows and the paintwork's flaking.

The town itself is okay, I suppose. There's an indoor shopping center, a movie theater, a soccer field, and a park with a skate ramp. In the central square, a spooky-looking, fifteenth-century abbey stands out against the sky. And behind the abbey, right at the edge of town, is a massive power station, empty at the moment, that's just been built for some kind of electricity conversion.

Our new home, the Old Vicarage, is about five minutes from the beach. It's a sturdy stone place, set back from the road behind a gravel driveway and iron gates. Mum says it's Victorian. Sometimes I think I see dark shapes flitting from roof to roof. Only seagulls, I suspect. Or cats. But I'm starting to feel surrounded by shadows.

And that name — Firecroft Bay. I wondered about it at first, but it's got nothing to do with fire. I looked it up, and it comes from the Old English, *firencræft*, which means "wickedness." In the bad sense. What does that mean? What wickedness happened here? I keep thinking about it.

I miss my old home, but we're not going back. London's in the past now and our new life is here, even though Dad never will be.

I'm not sure how I feel about it, but I'm living with it.

CHAPTER TWO

ice

THE OLD VICARAGE: MONDAY 08:10

"Have a good day, my love."

Mum gives me a hug in the hallway. Nobody to see us — well, only Truffle from his high chair in the kitchen — so I let her, without pulling away. I'm tired this morning, didn't sleep well again last night.

I look at my slim silver watch. Knowing the day and the time and where I am is important to me. Kind of helps me get a handle on the world around me. And the watch was my last ever birthday present from Dad. I wear it all the time.

"The bus leaves in ten minutes," I say. It's two miles up the coast to school. Where I used to live, the school was just a couple of streets from our front door and everyone knew everyone else.

Not like that here. I've got to start afresh.

"You'll make a lot of new friends," Mum says, "so look at it as an opportunity."

I look into her eyes. They're tired and crinkled, and her hair is starting to turn gray. She's had it cut short in a bob. If you look at the photos of her a year ago — when Dad was still alive — she's got a young, smooth face and long, chestnut-brown hair. She looks like a different person now. She doesn't talk much about all the stuff that brought us here, though. And she's trying to see the opportunity, too: She already has appointments booked, people wanting her "holistic therapy" — alternative healing treatments.

I shrug. "It's only school. What can go wrong?"

THE ESPLANADE: MONDAY 08:20

There's a cluster of kids in blue blazers and ties already huddled in the bus shelter. I grab the straps of my rucksack and try to make my eyes look hard. Straightaway I feel out of place because I haven't got my uniform yet; I'm in some boring jeans and a plain hoodie. I squirm inside, but nobody even looks in my direction.

Though it's late April now and there's pale sunlight, there's still a chilly wind. The sea's gray and choppy. Deckchair Man's setting out his stall, looking hopeful. I met him yesterday. He waves to me, and I wave back.

"Why are you waving?" says a tall girl standing next to me. Her voice is cold. She has a pointy face and sharp green eyes, and she wears her bright red hair in a long, elegant French braid on one side. She looks older than me. "And you're squinting."

I feel myself blushing. "I'm not."

"Yes, you are. You look like a ferret."

"Do ferrets squint?" I ask lightly, trying to ignore her rudeness.

She shrugs. "No idea." She holds out one long arm and shakes my hand. That's weird, formal. Like she's my mum's age. "I'm

Callista McGovern. Call me Cal. You're new, aren't you?"

"Miranda May. Just starting today."

I'm going to say more, but the bus arrives. The doors open with a *pssssht*, and there's a lot of pushing and shoving as the bigger boys get on first. I find myself right at the back of the line and only just manage to get on board before the doors close. The bus rattles and thumps off down the seafront road.

I hang on desperately, trying not to knock the other kids with my rucksack. The bus is close and airless and smells of bad aftershave, minty gum, and cheap perfume. But even with all those bodies packed in around me, I still feel cold. Why is that?

"You'll like the school," says Cal, who's straphanging beside me. "Eventually." She sounds very haughty and knowing, and doesn't look me in the eye as she speaks.

Why is she even bothering to talk to me if she doesn't like me? It's my first day — I just want keep my head down.

"Right," I say uncertainly.

A girl a few rows in front twists around in her seat to stare at me. She looks about ten. Bony and thin, blonde ponytail. I stare back, but she's got these intense eyes that make me sort of shrink inside. I look away.

But she's not the only one interested in the new girl. A boy sitting near her is texting but keeps glancing up at me. Again and again. It's like a nervous tic. His hair is so fair it's like a halo of white, and he's wearing blue-tinted glasses and a duffle coat, of all things. He seems about my age.

I look out of the window, away from the curious gazes. The bus lurches and judders on — hugging the old smugglers' bay, past a pub called the Barrel of Rum. It turns in a tight circle by the lighthouse, on the farthest-out spit of land, and begins to head slowly uphill into town.

Then I notice something strange: It's so cold I can see my breath.

The boys at the back of the bus have stopped jostling and thumping each other, and are now shivering and doing up their jackets.

"Is it always so *cold* here?" I say to Cal. "It's supposed to be April."

"No," says Cal thoughtfully. Her palm is pressed flat against the window. "It's not always this cold." She scrapes one finger down the wall of the bus and holds it up. The tip of her finger is coated with tiny white crystals. "Ice," she murmurs, and turns to look at a floppy-haired boy sitting behind us, holding her finger out toward him. "Josh?" she says, her voice questioning.

He gives her a sharp look, then pulls his iPod earphones out of his ears and stands up quickly. I guess he's a couple of years older than me.

The temperature in the bus has dropped even further, biting like a winter's day; everyone's looking at each other, pulling blazers and coats tightly around themselves. Through a clear patch in the window I can see it's still sunny outside; people are walking along without coats. But my face is turning numb.

And the bus is *creaking*.

"Look!" says Ponytail Girl. "Look at the ceiling."

Everyone on the bus looks up.

The ceiling is puckering and sparkling like the roof of an ice cave, and blue-white stalactites are starting to form, sprouting like living things from the metal roof. The windows are frosting, cracking, splintering.

The world seems to go into slow motion. Reality has shifted. I feel as if I am at the heart of an ice storm, everything whipping and swirling around me, and yet I'm miles away from it all.

"Whoa," I hear Cal say. "Ice, ice, *baby*."

I blink, and I'm snapped back into the real world.

It's really happening. The bus is covered, inside and out, with gleaming ice.

The boy named Josh turns, runs to the front, and bangs on the wall behind the driver.

"Stop!" he yells. "Stop this bus!" He turns toward Cal, his face deadly serious. "We've got to clear the bus. Get everyone out *now!*"

The bus driver brakes sharply, swings his cab door open, and jumps down.

"What are you kids going on about?" he snarls. "When I get to that school I'm gonna —" He stops abruptly as he sees what's happening all around him. "Crikey," he says in a small voice.

Cal pushes past him and slams her fist on the emergency door control. The doors squeal and grind, then spring open with a shattering of ice.

"Come on, rabble!" Cal orders. "Everyone off, quickly and quietly."

Rabble? I can't help thinking. Honestly, what an arrogant cow.

But everyone obeys. That's weird — like Cal has some natural authority beyond her age. They don't get off quickly and quietly, though. There's a panicked scramble, and for a moment I am swept along in the hordes of blue-blazered kids, my feet skidding. Just as I'm about to lose my balance, a hand grabs me and pulls me to the side. I look up and see Josh looking down at me through his floppy hair. I manage to smile in thanks, but he doesn't smile back. There is something hard about his blue eyes. Like Cal, I think. Just like Cal.

And what's Cal doing, now everyone's off the bus? She's scraping some ice off the window with a penknife. Then she puts it into what looks like a small specimen jar and slips that into her pocket.

"Come on, you lot!" shouts the driver from the door. "I gotta report this to the depot. And you're walking to school!"

Outside, the warmth of the spring day hits me, but the bus is still freezing over. The bright paintwork is disappearing beneath a layer of thick ice. It's as if the whole thing is turning into a solid block. Pupils have gathered in a crowd to watch, their jaws hanging open. Motorists and passersby slow down to stare.

It's unbelievable. I've never seen anything like it.

Then I see Josh, Cal, Ponytail Girl, and Duffle-coat Boy standing together, away from everyone else. They're talking quietly, but with a kind of . . . energy. *That's an odd group*, I think suddenly. A strange mix. What can they have in common? Then I get it. The energy . . .

They're excited.

I get a shiver down my spine, which I know has nothing to do with the ridiculously cold bus. It's just the feeling that this morning is the start of something big, something that's going to change my life forever.

KING EDWARD VI HIGH SCHOOL: MONDAY 08:55

Nothing like a good near disaster for starting the morning. Makes the whole rigmarole of standing in assembly, being gawked at, and finding my way around a bit easier to bear.

Everyone's talking about it in the corridors. You can hear it as you hurry past them *Yak-yak yak.*

"They said it was a blizzard. Snowin' inside the bus!"

"I heard they couldn't *see.*"

"Yeah, I heard their *eyelids* was frozen up!"

"Nah, I heard they got trapped inside by the ice and had to dig their way out with a rusty Coke can."

My homeroom teacher is Miss Bellini. I like her straightaway. She's tall and black and striking, with high cheekbones, perfect white teeth, and trendy designer glasses. Her cropped hair is a bit "mad professor," sticking out in random spikes, but I get the feeling she pays a lot of money for it to be like that.

"Just find yourselves a place, everyone," she says as we pile into the room. Her accent sounds American. For a moment, I think her

11

eyes settle on me, as if she is watching me carefully, sizing me up. And then the moment is gone. Perhaps I imagined it.

I find myself sitting next to a girl with tangled black hair, big hooped earrings, pierced nose, panda-eyes going on with the eyeliner. She's not wearing a uniform, either. Somehow, she's got away with coming to school in a battered JumpJets concert hoodie, frayed denim shorts, black diamond-patterned tights, and Goth-type boots with buckles. Looks cool, kind of Eastern European, like a Gypsy, maybe. She must be new as well.

In front of me sits the ponytail girl from the bus. What's *she* doing in my class? She seems much too young.

Gypsy Girl sees me looking. She puts a hand up to cover her mouth.

"See her?" she whispers, nodding in Ponytail Girl's direction.

"Yes?" I whisper back.

"Alyssa-Mae Myers. Lyssa, she calls herself. She's only nine, right? But she, like, got moved up after she found the stuff at her primary school too easy, yeah? Before she was seven, she'd rewritten the times table. And she got her General Certificate in Math in her spare time and made up a new language for fun."

"Sounds like a loser," I whisper, glaring at Lyssa's blonde ponytail.

"That's just the thing. She ain't. She's just a normal kid. Likes roller skating and bowling and that. Lives in public housing, a cheap flat with her mum." She pauses. "But there is somethin' a bit odd about her."

12

No kidding. I file the information for future use.

"I'm Miranda," I say to Gypsy Girl.

She nods. "Jade."

"Your class schedules!" says Miss Bellini. "Please pay attention. It would be embarrassing for you to end up in the wrong place. . . ."

MONDAY 12:47

I hurry along the corridor, eyes down. I seem to be going in a different direction from everyone else. I glance up for a second and see, at the end of the corridor, floppy hair. It's Josh. He's on his own, his back to me, and he's talking quietly into a cell phone. I edge closer.

". . . we need to talk," I hear. "And get that sample analyzed right now. Chemistry lab's free."

He snaps the phone shut and slips it into his pocket. Then he looks up and sees me.

"Hello," I say.

"Not lost already?" he says coolly.

"No, no. Just . . ." I look around for inspiration. ". . . checking out the netball club bulletin board. I might join."

"Oh, *sports*. Yes, all right if you like that kind of thing, I suppose."

"Well, I do," I say.

Jade has told me all about this guy, too. Josh Barnes, refugee from private school when his dad lost all his money.

We fall into silence. He looks down at me, just as he did on the bus, and then his blue eyes seem to sharpen.

I take a step backward.

Okay, so *that* feels strange. He's not looking at me like he fancies me or wants to snog me or anything. Well, I could cope with that. I'd tell him where to go. (Yes, I would.) No, it's weirder than that. He looks almost . . . puzzled.

"Interesting," he says eventually, and it's only then that I realize I've been holding my breath. "I thought so on the bus. Low-level and basic, but you *are* . . ."

I take another step backward. "What are you talking about?"

"Here's some advice, Miranda," he says. "Keep your head down, and if anyone asks you what happened on the bus, you say you've no idea, right?"

Before I can ask him how he knows my name, and tell him that I really *don't* have a clue what happened on the bus, he turns and saunters off in the direction of the quad, hands in pockets.

When the bell rings out for the end of lunch, I jump a mile.

What did he mean, "you are"?

I am *what*?

CHAPTER THREE

seaview

THE OLD VICARAGE: MONDAY 15:55

"Did you have a good first day?" asks my mother, placing a cup of strong, steaming tea on the wooden kitchen table in front of me.

I look up at her in gratitude. "Not bad, thanks, Mum."

I don't always drink tea — it tastes quite bitter to me — but the mug warms my cold hands. And there is something loving about tea, despite its bitterness, something comforting and Saturday-autumn-evening. It reminds me of cuddling up to Dad and watching the soccer results or *Britain's Got Talent*.

Mum sits opposite me at the table. As usual, various books and papers are scattered in front of her. Truffle's taking a nap.

"Your pop magazine's arrived," she says, pushing *Rolling Stone* over to me.

I smile indulgently. *Your pop magazine.* She always calls it that. I've given up trying to change her.

Her pen scratches across the pages of her notebook, and I leaf through the pages of my magazine. No JumpJets news that I can see. Barometric are splitting up — well, no surprises there, Sherlock, as they all hate each other. I found out from their website days ago. And MC Salacious is slated to remix the Calvino Brothers' new single. That's going to sound *rubbish*.

Mum sighs and pushes her glasses up on the top of her head. "Did you meet anyone nice?" she asks.

I shrug. "A few people."

"What's your homeroom teacher like? Miss Bellini, isn't it?"

"She's okay. Quite strict, in a quiet way. But nice."

Mum puts down her pen for a moment and folds her hands. "Miranda," she says, and the way she says my name makes me fold my *Rolling Stone* shut and sit up.

"Yes, Mum?"

"You would tell me, wouldn't you," she says, "if anything . . . odd happened at school? Anything that made you feel uncomfortable?"

You mean like the school bus freezing up for no reason in the middle of April, Mum? Is that the kind of thing you had in mind? You mean like a weird older boy peering into my eyes and telling me that I'm something, I don't know what?

I don't want to tell her about Josh, but I know she'll hear about the bus incident. It'll be all around town soon. I try to sound casual.

"Oh, the bus broke down and we had to walk. It was weird, actually. I think the . . . thermostat broke or something? The driver wasn't very happy."

Mum smiles, then hesitates, as if weighing something up. "You're so important to me, Miranda," she says finally. "So important in so many ways. Just . . . be careful."

16

She disappears upstairs to check on Truffle, but her words echo in my head, as if they carry some sort of strange meaning I don't yet know.

CRAGHOLLOW PARK: MONDAY 17:34

I'm wandering around the park on my own, skateboarding, listening to my iPod, and wondering if I'm ever going to have any friends. And feeling pretty miserable. Trying to do some flips on the skate ramp and getting them wrong.

To my surprise, I see Jade, who sat next to me in class. She's on the wooden carousel, pushing out with her foot so that she spins gently. She's chewing, and watching me with an amused grin. As she catches my eye, she offers me some chewing gum. Cautiously, I go up to her and take it. I nod at her. She nods back. For a few moments, we don't say anything.

"You ain't bad with that," she says eventually, nodding at the skateboard.

Blushing, I sit down beside her. "Yeah, well, got to practice a bit more. Not used to this ramp. You from London?" I say. "I didn't get a chance to ask."

"Yeah," says Jade.

"Me too. Where?" I ask.

"Lewisham," she says. "You?"

"We used to live in Cricklewood," I say.

She grins. "So what brought you to this dump?"

"Well, it was for my mum's work," I say, not wanting to elaborate. "How about you?"

She shrugs, doesn't look at me. "This and that," she says, and gazes into the distance, chewing, as if not quite sure whether she trusts me.

There's a pause.

"You got away with that JumpJets top in school."

She grins, looking down at it. "Yeah, but I won't again. Miss Bellini told me that."

"Did you go to the free gig in Trafalgar Square?" I ask. This is the only time I've seen my favorite band. A four-song set as part of a radio station's charity day. Uncle Jeff and his girlfriend took me. Mum doesn't really let me go to actual concerts yet.

Jade looks at me and grins. "Was you really there?"

"Yeah."

"Wow, we was both there. And now we're both here. How weird is that?"

After five minutes, we are talking freely. And after two hours, we are almost like old friends. Her full name's Giada-Divina Verdicchio. She has to spell it for me. It's Italian.

So as the sun sets I spend time walking around Firecroft Bay with Giada — Jade. Eating chips, looking at the shops and the bright amusement arcades, and thinking how different it all feels from London. How alien. And I don't like that pungent, dead smell.

"People used to think it was ozone," I say to Jade. "Like air full of oxygen, really good for you — but no, it's just rotting seaweed."

"Yuck," she says. "Rotting seaweed, fish and chips, and cotton candy."

"Yeah, that's the smell of Firecroft Bay. Nice, huh?"

"Gross."

Jade says people have told her the place comes alive in a few weeks when the tourists descend with their dribbling ice creams and screaming tots. Can't wait. Not.

But at least I've got a friend who likes the same music.

Everything would be looking up if it weren't for the oddness with the bus, and those four weird kids who acted like they know something about me.

And the Shape, of course. Always the Shape.

KING EDWARD VI HIGH SCHOOL: WEDNESDAY 15:15

Home time. Freedom. We're pouring out of the doors, down the steps, and across the playground, a great river of babbling, laughing, shouting kids and all the other stuff that goes with us: swinging bags, untucked shirts, chucked apple cores, coats thrown and dragged.

My uniform's arrived, so I don't stick out as much. And I've started to get into a routine. I can almost swan through the gate now, rucksack slung casually. I can loosen my tie, make out like I belong here. That's the key. That's how you avoid being noticed, avoid being bullied. I can do fake confidence, I tell myself. I have to. Got to put on a show for the world, even though I'm dying inside.

But I don't talk about my dad. Not even to Jade, not yet.

She's waiting at the gate for me now. She's wearing bright lipstick, giant earrings, and her tie big-knotted halfway down with about three shirt buttons open. She's chewing gum, and her eyes are hidden behind shades. Some boy says something rude to her and she snaps back a response, flicking the finger at him. I smile and pick up my pace.

And then I spot them.

It's the first time since the bus that I've seen them all together. All sitting on top of a bench like starlings on a telephone wire. Everybody else is giving them a wide berth, as if there's an exclusion zone around them.

Josh Barnes, gangly and floppy-haired, in a long, dark coat that looks too big for him. I haven't spotted him since that weird conversation in the corridor. Would he even go to the trouble of avoiding me? Cal McGovern, leaning intently forward, her flaming hair bright in the April sun. Lyssa Myers, scowling like I've just stolen her favorite One Direction pencil. And the boy with shaggy white-blond hair and tinted specs. He's listening to something on earphones, tapping one finger on the palm of his hand. I've found out his name now. It's Oliver "Ollie" Hanwell.

They are all looking at me.

I want to confront them. I want to say, *What's your problem?* Bit of Jade-attitude, perhaps. But I'm still a newbie here. I'm just getting to know the ropes. I've made it this far without getting any trouble, and I don't intend to start now.

Casting one last, nervous look over my shoulder, I join Jade at the gate.

"All right?" she says.

"Yeah, not bad."

I tap her left earring. "Studs only, it says in the rules."

She grins. "When you're me, babe, you can get away with any- thing." She senses my gaze drifting to the group on the bench. "Weirdos," she says. "Don't worry about them."

"Why are they all hanging out together?"

Jade shrugs. "I dunno. Do you really give a toss? Just what weirdos do, innit? Come on, let's go down to the Esplanade."

I follow her, out of the gate and along the school fence.

My mind isn't on our conversation, though. Sunlight flickers in and out of the metal fence posts, strobing in my eyes. I'm sure I can still feel four pairs of eyes drilling into me all the way down the hill, past the tiled roofs, and toward the misty seafront. Eyes inside my head.

* * *

So I start to watch them back.

Lyssa Myers is one top genius. They weren't joking. Take Chemistry, where she sits right at the front, and knows the answer to *everything*.

Like this: "Hydrogen chloride, miss!"

Or this: "Sublimation, miss!"

See what I mean?

Her arm goes up and down like a yo-yo. She seems to know

the answers to the questions before Miss Bellini has even finished asking them.

Today Miss Bellini starts class like a conjuror, producing four Ping-Pong balls from nowhere — two red ones in her left hand, and two blue ones in her right.

Everyone gasps. Except Jade, who says, *"Ta-dah!"* sarcastically, and makes everyone laugh, including Miss Bellini.

"Just like that!" says Miss Bellini with a grin, then she slams the four balls into one another. They stick together in one blue and red mass. "Now then . . . Miranda May."

I sit bolt upright. "Miss?"

Jade kicks me under the table. "Watch out," she mutters.

"Catch!" she says, and throws the model to me.

I catch it. Smart. Netball practice coming in useful.

"Good!" says Miss Bellini, nodding. "Now . . . can you name me something whose nucleus looks like that? Hmm?" She peers over her glasses at me. "Which element?"

"Um . . ."

I'm thinking hard. I know this. We did it only the other day.

"Give you a clue," says Miss Bellini. "It makes you *talk like this!*" And she does a squeaky, high-pitched voice, which makes everyone fall about laughing. "Okay, okay!" she says, holding out her hands, and the hubbub subsides as if by magic. She nods at me again. "Miranda?"

I've got it, of course. "Helium, miss."

"Helium. Yes."

And Miss Bellini smiles at me.

And that's how I get by, in general. I'm tired because of the dream, because of not sleeping, but in school I'm pretty normal. I'm okay at Science, good at Math and English, keep my trap shut in History, and get by in French. *Jean-Paul est dans le jardin*, etc., etc. Yeah, yeah. Wake me up when Jean-flipping-Paul does something exciting.

THURSDAY 14:15

Okay, I've decided I don't like being watched. And they're still watching me. I know they are. I need to work out what is going on, before it drives me crazy. So I've made a plan.

At afternoon break, I spot Ollie Hanwell disappearing down the corridor in his duffle coat. You can see his bright blond hair a mile off. Just as I'm about to go after him, Jade's beside me. "All right, mate?" She takes me by the elbow. "C'mon, what you skulking round here for?"

"Um, I've got . . . something to do. Sorry."

"Ooh, secret mission. You *meeting* someone?"

"No, not like that."

"Oh, yeah?" She grins expectantly, swiveling on one heel. "Who's lover-boy? You got someone waiting to snog you round by the Biology labs?"

"Five minutes," I say, holding up a hand. "Just gimme five minutes."

I shoot off through the double doors at the top of the corridor.

I run at full tilt past the language lab and the classrooms, and skid at the end so I almost lose my balance. Breathless, I pound down the stairs, jumping the last three, and turn the corner — just in time to see Ollie disappear toward the sports fields. I hurry after him.

I find him on the bench by the track, putting on his rugby cleats. I sit near to him, glancing up to see if he has noticed me, and open the packet of mints I have in my pocket.

"Chilly this afternoon," I say.

He looks up, narrows his eyes as if trying to place me, then smiles. "Oh, it's *you*. Miranda, isn't it?"

So he knows my name, too. Have the Weirdos been talking about me as well as watching me?

I wonder whether to mention the watching. I decide not to, for now. Better to be cool and remote. Play them at their own game.

"Like the bag," I say.

"Really?" He looks worried, as if he's wondering whether I'm mocking him. Not surprising, really, as it's just a normal sports bag.

"I've been looking for one like that. Where did you get it?"

"Umm . . . I can't remember," he says, concentrating on tying his cleats. "Do you mind? I've . . . got stuff to do, here."

I hold up my hands. "Sorry. Don't mind me."

He nods. "Okay. Well. See you around," he says, looking at me curiously one last time.

"Sure." I wave at him as he disappears to rugby.

As soon as he's out of sight around the corner, I slip my hand into his bag and find what I'm looking for. Then I allow myself to breathe out. And I hurry off, late, to French, feeling the slim, smooth shape of Ollie Hanwell's cell phone tucked into my inside blazer pocket.

Mission accomplished.

THE OLD VICARAGE: THURSDAY 16:05

Stealing? What do you mean, *stealing*?

It's more complicated than that. I have a plan. I'm going to find out what this is all about. Because ever since I came here, a lot of things have not been making sense. And things not making sense churns me up inside, makes my heart pound faster, and my body feel tense, aching. I need to do something. I can't do anything about the Shape and the dream, but I can get to the bottom of why those four Weirdos keep looking at me. And if, ahem, *borrowing* a phone is what it takes, then that's what I have to do.

I'll give it back.

Just as soon as I've got the information I need.

Mum's feeding Truffle. He's sitting in his chair with some sort of apple concoction around his mouth, and he opens his eyes wide as I plonk my bag on the kitchen table.

"Hi, Mum. Hi, Truffle."

"*Manja!*" says Truffle delightedly, and points at me.

Mum, her hair all over the place and her glasses pushed up on top of her head, pauses with the spoon halfway to Truffle's mouth. "Tash is coming round at five," she says. "I have to be out visiting the old people's home. A few clients there."

This is the sort of thing my mum does all the time. I've been used to a succession of "helpers," as she calls them, coming in to look after me and Truffle. Tash must be the latest.

"I've got to go out in a bit," I say. "Need to . . . collect some shells."

"Shells?" says Mum.

"For . . . Science. A project," I say, trying to sound vague but also as if I've given her a full and complete answer.

It's not easy, lying to Mum.

"Well, okay," she says, but she gives me a strange look.

I rush upstairs, my feet thumping on the steps, crash into my room, and flop onto the bed.

Then I pull out Ollie's phone, thumb it on, and start checking the texts. It's intrusive. I feel guilty. But I'm a detective now. Pretty soon, he's going to notice it's missing, and he'll do what I'd do — phone his own number and see who answers. I'd like to think I wouldn't be daft enough to answer, but you never know.

Five minutes later, I've got the information I need. I change into a top and leggings, grab my favorite leather jacket. I thump down the stairs again.

In the hall, I lace my Doc Martens. I pause, grab my battered old skateboard. Why not? I need to travel quickly.

"See you later, Mum!"

I slam the front door behind me and I don't hear what she says in response.

For a second I look out across the crooked, tiled roofs that

26

sweep down toward the harbor. From up here, the sea is a vast blue-gray monster fringed with white, like lace, and the calls of gulls echo up in the clouds as if mocking me. The place seems colder today, more threatening somehow. Like the harbor is a trap.

Shivering, I banish these thoughts, zip up my jacket, and hop on the board, then skim toward the shore, the opening blast of "Emotional Vandal" (first track on the JumpJets' debut album *We Will Be Back After This Short Intermission*) pounding through my headphones.

ESPLANADE: THURSDAY 16:31

It doesn't take long to find the Seaview Hotel.

I'm amazed the text on Ollie's phone mentioned it by name, but here it is, and here I am. I check my watch, pull my scarf up over the bottom half of my face, and crouch behind a builder's dumpster opposite the front of the hotel. I hide my skateboard in the dumpster, as I don't want to be encumbered with it when I get inside.

The hotel looks as if it was grand once. It looms above the seafront like a castle, towers and crenellations reaching up into the sky. It's old and battered now, though, and covered in moss and lichen. Seagulls whirl around it like castle ravens. Some windows are covered with metal grilles; others are boarded up and defaced with rude graffiti. Across the front of the building are faded iron letters saying "SEA I W HO EL." (Someone wanted to make a sign saying "VET," then.) There's litter in the doorway — Coke

27

cans, candy wrappers — and the door itself is battered and peeling.

Someone's striding along the Esplanade in my direction. It's Josh.

I duck behind the dumpster and watch. He's got his collar turned up against the cold wind, and he checks quickly behind him before hurrying up the steps of the hotel. I think he swipes some sort of card in the lock and the door clicks open. I wait two seconds, watching as the old wooden door starts to swing shut behind Josh. Then I quickly look up and down the seafront road, dash across to the hotel, and scamper up the steps.

I don't make it in time. The door clicks shut.

"D'oh!"

Okay. I think for a minute, and then I have an idea.

I get my library card out and slip it in between the catch and the door frame. I jiggle it up and down, ear to the door like a safe-cracker. I listen for Josh's footsteps receding and, when I think it's safe, I twist the card, press the door lightly — and it opens.

Cool, right? I got that from *Burgle My House!* There's a reality show for everything these days.

I slip inside and pull the door closed behind me.

It slams shut and I jump, wincing. Did anyone hear?

I wait. Silence.

I'm in an old-fashioned hotel lobby, dimly lit and covered in cobwebs. Huge cobwebs. I don't want to think about how big the spiders were that made them. And it's dusty, too — I have to put a finger over my nose to stop myself sneezing. There's a wooden reception desk with a rusty bell, and a huge staircase leading up into darkness. At the back there's an old elevator with one of those metal lattice gates on it — and it's making a soft whining sound.

I tiptoe across the lobby. Above the elevator is a dial. The pointer has stopped at LG, for Lower Ground floor.

Okay. I know where Josh has gone. So do I risk taking the elevator myself? My finger hovers over the button but I think better of it. Beside the elevator there's a fire door. I ease it open — it creaks alarmingly — and find two flights of stone steps, one leading up and the other down.

For a moment I shiver as cold air wafts up toward me. But I tell myself to get a grip. There's a mystery here, and I'm not going to solve it by standing around doing nothing. And I need to know. It burns, it almost hurts. Why me? Why them? Why now, and here? I make my way down.

The stairs stop in what looks like an empty underground parking lot. All I can see are concrete walls, chunky pillars, scattered newspapers, and drink cans. There's even an abandoned, blackened barbecue.

And then I spot something. A metal door, ajar, on the far side, hidden in the shadows. I sidle toward it, push it open, and slip into the darkness beyond. I'm on some sort of gantry. I look down, and take a sharp breath at what I see.

Below me is an expanse of white stone floor, lit dimly by some source I can't see. Gantries, like the one I'm on, crisscross at different levels, with metal staircases leading down to a space that looks like a mix of lab, crypt, factory floor, and messy living room.

The dark walls are curved, and on one is a matte blackboard, covered with photos and notes. On another is a spotlit map — I think it's Firecroft Bay. Desks of different heights are piled with junk: gutted computers, old-fashioned radios, circuit boards, papers, maps. I spot a chessboard, a click-clacking Newton's Cradle and, bizarrely, a full-size pool table. One desk is draped in a huge, spaghetti-like bundle of . . . what are those things called? We saw them in school once. Fiber-optic cables, that's it. Twinkling like Christmas lights and sending a flickery blue glow over the room.

I drop to my knees and crawl a little farther. Now I really have to stop myself from gasping. Because there, in her lab coat, expensive glasses, and wild hair, writing on a clipboard, is Miss Bellini.

"No sign of any fluid leakage at all?" she says in her rich voice, and from my new vantage point I realize who she's talking to: Josh, leaning against a desk, and Cal, sitting with her feet up on a computer and filing her nails.

"Nothing, Miss B," says Cal. "A real puzzle." She takes something out of her pocket and hands it to Miss Bellini — a small glass phial. "Just water," she says. "Nothing weird."

Miss Bellini holds it up to the light. "Got to be *something* weird about it, Callista," she says. "It came outta nowhere."

"Some sort of molecular stimulation?" says a chirpy voice. It's little genius girl Lyssa Myers, sitting in the shadows, cross-legged on a chair. "A hidden catalyst causing a high-velocity chemical change?"

I have absolutely *no* idea what she is talking about.

No change there, then.

My heart's beating faster. There's something strange going on here. And whatever it is, they're all in on it. But what's it got to do with the way they were staring at me?

"But it's just ice," says Ollie. "Pure, simple ice."

Yup, he's there, too — white-blond Ollie with his hands in his pockets, strolling up and down.

I can see something else now. On a computer screen in the center of the room is a 3-D image of the unmistakable, chunky form of the frozen school bus.

I shift position slightly to get a better look. And that's when it happens.

In the near darkness, I knock something with my foot. A soccer ball, up here on the gantry. It rolls and thumps along the metal bridge as my hand flies to my mouth, and goes *thump-thumpy-thumpy-thumpy-BUMP* down the stairs.

Now I'm done for.

I see Josh step forward and scoop the ball up in one swift move, like a practiced goalie.

"Who's there?" he calls up. "Come out!"

Right. Time to get out of here.

Still crouching, I turn, ready to make my escape the way I came in. But just as I turn to the metal door behind me, it snaps shut with an echoing *CLANG!* blocking off my only escape route.

I suppose there's no point trying to hide anymore.

31

I straighten up nervously and emerge from the shadows to face them.

"Um . . . hello," I say, and I give them what I hope is a friendly wave.

They stand at the bottom of the stairs in a semicircle, looking up — Lyssa Myers smiling unnervingly, Josh leaning against the wall, bouncing the soccer ball and looking disapproving, Cal with her hands on her hips and a frown on her face, and Ollie with his head to one side, looking at me as if he's sure he's seen me somewhere before.

"Hello, Miranda," says Miss Bellini, folding her arms.

"Sorry, miss," I say in a small voice.

But to my surprise, all she does is put her hand out in a welcoming gesture.

"Why don't you come down?" she says. "After all — we've been expecting you."

CHAPTER FOUR

shadows

SO WHAT DO I DO? I CAN'T TURN AND RUN. I CAN'T phone for help. I have to make my way slowly down the stairs, into the lion's den.

My DMs clang and echo on the metal stairs.

They are all looking at me. My heart is thumping like mad, and I'm really wishing now that I'd told someone — Mum or Jade — where I was going. I look at them one by one — Josh, Cal, Lyssa, Ollie — and remind myself that I know them.

Miss Bellini pulls out a black, padded swivel chair and spins it around. "Have a seat," she says.

I sit down cautiously on the leather chair. High above, near the dark ceiling, I'm sure I can hear pigeons fluttering and cooing. I realize now that the secret place I am in stretches all the way to the top of the hotel, the floors in between having rotted away or maybe having been removed.

"What do you mean, you were expecting me?" I ask.

Cal tosses her red hair. "Just that," she says. "You didn't need to come in by . . . well, it was hardly 'stealth.' You could have just rung the front doorbell."

"You can't have known I was coming," I snap.

Miss Bellini turns to Ollie. "Perhaps you'd like to put Miss May out of her misery, Ollie."

Ollie grins, and starts to empty his duffle-coat pockets onto a metal table. "Hang on just a minute . . ." A yo-yo is followed by a roll of mints, some chewing gum, and some StarBreaker trading cards. That's . . . almost unnervingly normal. "Aha!" he says at last, and fishes out what looks like a small silver stopwatch. "Tracker," he says. "Following the bug inside my phone. So we, ah, knew where you were."

"I knew without that," says Cal sniffily.

"Oh, well." Ollie shrugs. "Yeah. You did say you knew she'd come."

What is this? I've read that you can buy bugs and hidden cameras and things off the Internet, but they cost, what, thousands? And Cal *knew* I'd come? What's that all about?

I suddenly feel very stupid. "Oliver, you . . . *let* me steal your phone?"

Ollie smiles. "'Course!" he says. "I mean, you didn't think you'd actually swiped it, did you? Don't mean to be rude, Miranda, but a limping elephant could have done it more subtly. Could I have it back now, please?"

Realizing the game is up, I sigh and hand Ollie back his phone. He takes it with a friendly grin and a nod of thanks.

"This . . . place," I say cautiously. "It's abandoned, right?"

"Used to be the Seaview Hotel," says Cal, leaning against the pool table. She offers me some chewing gum. I hesitate, and she waggles it. "Go on, for goodness' sake. We're hardly going to try and poison you."

I take the stick of chewing gum carefully and fold it into my mouth, its powdery texture softening as I turn it around with my tongue.

"This," says Josh, waving his arm around, "was the biggest and best hotel in Firecroft Bay, until . . . well, until it wasn't."

"Tell Miranda the real reason," says Miss Bellini quietly. She is watching us all with amusement, twirling her glasses.

Josh grins. "Well, I didn't want to scare our guest. But, yes, there was an . . . incident a good few years back. The owner fell several floors to her death. Or was she pushed? Nasty. Horrible mess." He winces, tut-tuts. "It was never solved. Nobody really wanted to stay here after that. Some people say that, at night, you can still hear her screaming."

I fold my arms and meet Josh's gaze coolly, trying to show him I'm not unsettled by this. Even though I am.

"Anyway," he goes on, "it stood empty for a few years, and we decided it would be a good place for a base."

"A *base*?" I say. "What are you, then, the Fantastic Four? The Famous Five? Or have you just been watching too much *Scooby-Doo*?" I look over at Miss Bellini, who is clicking her pen against her clipboard. "Miss?"

Miss Bellini strolls over to the illuminated map and taps it. "You may joke, Miranda. But the whole of this area of the British coastline is steeped in myths, legends . . . unusual activities."

She clicks a button beside the map. Nothing happens at first. She gives it a thump, and tiny blue pin-lights spring into life.

Miss Bellini smiles. "Sorry about that. We're not that high-tech here. Have to salvage what we can from all kinds of sources. This map's forty years old, believe it or not."

The lights form lines, all intersecting in the center of the brown mass that represents Firecroft Bay.

"Ley lines?" I say, and I blush as they all turn to look at me.

Miss Bellini smiles. "Very good! Science and myth are not as far apart as some people like to claim."

"Really?" I can't help sounding skeptical.

"Of course!" Miss Bellini beams. "Ley lines, Miranda, are lines of power. Yes, the power is old, it's dark, and we don't fully understand it, but be assured, it is there. And, in some places — especially in Britain with all its legends and history — this power comes together. Like an electrical grid. Firecroft Bay is one of those places where ancient powers converge."

"Converge." All I seem able to do is repeat stuff.

Miss Bellini sweeps her hand across the map. "There are more sites of ancient historic interest — forts, tumuli, megaliths, and the like — per square mile here than anywhere else in England. Did you know that? And harbor towns are *special*. They have the energy of both the land and the sea. Things *happen* here which just shouldn't happen. Paranormal activity. Objects and people disappearing. All kinds of other . . . phenomena."

"Phenomena. Right." Doing it again. Pretty Polly. But I'm slowly trying to piece stuff together. Is she talking about things like my dreams? The Shape? The ice? That strange moment on the bus when I felt as if I wasn't really there?

Miss Bellini puts on her glasses and stares intently at me. "Oh, yes. Make no mistake, Miranda. This is an area of huge paranormal importance. Wherever there's a Convergence, reality becomes unstable. And here, the activity is getting stronger and stronger, day by day."

"Okaaaay," I say. Part of me is still wondering if, at any moment, someone's going to leap out with a microphone and a camera crew and tell me I've been caught by some stupid TV prank show. But another part of me knows what Miss Bellini's saying makes sense.

She looks around at the little group. "We haven't been doing this very long. I only arrived in Firecroft Bay myself last term. It wasn't difficult to find out which pupils of mine were . . . well, likely to be interested in these incidents. To take it all seriously."

The foursome are all looking at me in *that* way again. Half interested, half out to get me.

"So . . . what do you mean, *incidents?*"

Cal says, "Things happen here against the laws of nature."

"Disappearances," says Josh. "Shadows. Odd power surges. Ghosts. Things you sense out of the corner of your eye."

Cal slides up behind Josh and puts her chin on his shoulder. She whispers, "The things most people dismiss. But we don't dismiss them. We're learning how to . . . catch them."

"You guys totally weird me out," I say slowly. "You're telling me you're some sort of . . . secret team of spook-bashers?"

Miss Bellini gives me one of her big trademark smiles. "Everyone here is special, and here for a reason." She peers over her glasses. "Including *you*, Miranda May."

Josh leans down and claps me on the shoulder. "We see things we're not supposed to see," he says softly. "We know things we're not meant to know."

"Conspiracies," says Cal.

"Secrets," says Miss Bellini, "on the other side of madness — and at the borders of what you call reality."

"Me, I do the investigating," says Josh. "The history, the digging, the finding out of things people don't know, or don't want to be known." He nods at Cal, who's gone over to the pool table. "My red-haired friend here is the coordinator, good at making connections, reading people and objects, and being *intuitive*."

"And bossing you all about," says Cal as she lines up her shot. "Someone has to."

"Our little Lyssa." Josh puts an arm around her shoulders, and she looks up, smiling. "She's our genius. Math, languages, obscure bits of science. And Ollie's our tame geek and gadget boy. Keeps the computers fed, gets the pizzas delivered, and, er, makes bad jokes. Usually."

"But you're just a bunch of kids," I say doubtfully.

I mean, it's just daft. Ollie's in the same grade as me, Cal the

38

grade above. Josh, the oldest, is still only fifteen. And Lyssa, well, she'd be in elementary school if she didn't have a brain the size of Big Ben.

"Yup," says Josh.

"Rather helps, in fact," says Cal. She slides the cue with a smart flick of one hand, and sinks the eight ball. "*Yesss!*"

"You see," says Ollie, "once you know the weird and you *accept* it, you can move on — toward understanding it."

"And you're investigating what's happening?" I ask them.

"Like you say," says Cal, gesturing with her pool cue, "we're just a bunch of kids. And that makes us the perfect investigators. Undercover, underground, underhand."

"Underfunded," adds Miss Bellini over her shoulder. She's moved to a desk on one of the higher-up platforms, surrounded by computer keyboards and screens. I am about to ask who *does* pay for all this, but then something else happens.

"Put these on," says Lyssa, behind me, and before I can stop her she has slipped a pair of headphones over my ears.

"What's going on?" I ask, panicking.

"Only a little test, Miranda," says Miss Bellini with a reassuring smile. "Just want to confirm something."

I don't see why I should do this. They aren't holding me here by force. I could get up and leave right now if I wanted to.

But then I wouldn't have answers. And I'd have had a wasted journey.

I may even learn something by playing along. I lean back in the soft, enveloping leather chair and adjust the headphones so that they sit comfortably on my ears.

Ollie, from over by another computer screen, says, "It'll help if you close your eyes."

Okay. Nothing to lose.

Nervously, I let my eyelids close and realize that I am in need of sleep. I feel myself drifting almost immediately.

*   *   *

Is this dream or reality? It's like that odd time when you're waking up in the morning, and you only realize afterward that you were hearing conversations from the radio alarm, picturing them in your half dreams.

I think I open my eyes — do I? I can't tell, I am in darkness. I am alone. It's cold. Not just chilly, but depths-of-January freezing.

Something is wrong.

The Shape is here. Fire and water and darkness.

"Who are you?" I ask. I don't know if I ask this out loud, or just think it. Why haven't I asked this before?

The Shape does not respond. There's no whisper this time. But there is a whistling, an echoing tune. I know it, the tune . . . it's . . . it's . . .

I'm trying to remember it, to place it, but the Shape's growing bigger and bigger. No, I realize — not bigger, but closer. Coming toward me through a vortex of darkness.

Coming to get me. And now the whisper comes.

Miranda . . .

* * *

"*No!*" I shout, and my eyes snap open.

I'm back in the hotel basement again, and I'm standing, looking down at the chair where I've thrown the headphones.

I don't remember jumping up from the chair.

But the headphones are still rocking back and forth, so I must have dropped them just a few seconds ago.

"Josh?" says Miss Bellini, looking up from her clipboard.

I realize Josh is standing there with a stopwatch. "7.1 seconds," he says. "Not bad at all. Good assimilation."

"Lyssa?" says Miss Bellini.

"Intensity 44," says Lyssa. She's standing by a computer screen right next to me. "Wow."

Ollie nods. "Same reading over here."

"What is all this?" I snap. "What were you testing?"

"Interesting," says Lyssa. "I'd actually calculated a thirteen percent chance that she might fail." She looks at me mischievously.

"What did you see?" Cal asks, leaning forward. "Tell us."

I glower at her. "I'm not a test subject! I'm not some animal in a cage! Will you guys tell me what this is all *about*?"

"Josh," says Miss Bellini gently, "why don't you take Miranda for a little walk and explain everything? We can get on with analyzing the bus."

"He doesn't have to *take* me anywhere," I say. "I'm out of here."

I storm up the stairs, *clang-clang-clang*, hitting the door at the top with the flat of my hand so it stings. I'm half expecting the door not to open, but it does.

Into the abandoned parking lot and then back up into the decaying lobby of the Seaview Hotel, and in one, two, three, four steps I am out of the doors and onto the seafront again, breathing deep gulps of the seaweedy air.

The spring sun is bright, harsh in my eyes.

As I'm grabbing my skateboard I half hear someone shouting something after me, but I really don't care anymore. I'm striding again, burning with anger, my eyes fixed on the churning sea.

It's like I am moving in slow motion, with the jagged fans of spray caught on a camera, the seagulls circling above me as if they're about to attack me, and at the corner of my eye I see —

It's here. A column of shimmering darkness, there on the beach, beyond the Esplanade. Something the size of a human, but not human . . . outlined in fire . . . at the water's edge . . . And that whistling tune. In my head. I'm not asleep — I know I'm not. . . .

Without thinking, my eyes fixed on that half shadow on the beach, I am in the road.

A screaming, squealing sound.

A deafening klaxon.

A huge wall of metal and glass bearing down on me.

There's no way I can get out of its path.

And in that second, I know I'm about to die.

CHAPTER FIVE

decision

PROPELLED BY SOME FORCE, SOMETHING KICKING within me, I half jump, half throw myself to the edge of the road, slamming right up against a parked car as a huge truck thunders by at enormous speed, trailing a smell of hot exhaust and rubber. It doesn't even slow down, let alone stop, just hurtles on along the bay.

Bruised and dazed, my back aching where I bashed myself against the car, I try to pick myself up.

People have gathered around me. I'm shaking.

I'm trying to work out how I did that.

An old lady in a purple coat grabs my arm and helps me to stand. "Are you all right, love? What a bloomin' maniac! Some people oughtn't to be allowed on the roads!"

"Naaaah, she walked out in front of it!" says a man behind her, waving his cone. "Don't they teach road safety in them schools no more? Eh?"

"I . . . I'm fine," I say, giving the old lady a weak smile. "Really, I am."

And I am, really. Worse things have happened in my life, after all. But I'm still shaking.

"Are you okay?" says a familiar voice, and I feel a hand on my elbow. It's Josh.

So he followed me out, then. Sent by Miss Bellini, no doubt, or by Cal.

"Fine," I say, glowering at him. "It . . . it really wasn't anywhere near me."

Eventually, the oldies leave me alone — after a bit more clucking and fussing, and once they've been reassured by a charming Josh that I don't need an ambulance. I only think then to check my watch. I pull back my sleeve, heart pounding, but it's fine. Unbroken. It's pretty resilient in its tough chrome casing. I see it's just gone five. I can't stay out much longer without letting Mum know.

"Look," Josh says, "I'm sorry, okay? Come to the café. We'll talk."

I shrug. "Why?"

"Because you've got questions. And I've got a few answers."

He turns, starts walking back along the Esplanade. I watch him for a second or two. Then I curse quietly and hurry after him.

SEAFRONT CAFÉ, ESPLANADE: THURSDAY 17:05

So I'm sitting opposite Josh. This place has red plastic seats and tables, the specials chalked on old blackboards, a cheap-and-cheerful feel. Rain's beginning to speckle the windows and turn the sea hazy. Out on the Esplanade, people are struggling with umbrellas and shopping. Kids skateboard and roller-skate past.

The world carrying on despite it all.

And I've texted Mum to tell her where I am. In a café with friends. All quite normal. Tum-ti-tum. If only she knew. The sea mist is prowling the beach, and now and then curls of spray dash the pier. Deckchairs flap, their canvases pulled taut in the wind like parachutes.

It's as if the world is restless.

My head is spinning with all kinds of possibilities. I'm scared but . . . nervous. Excited, even. What's coming next?

Josh brings a tray from the counter. He puts a large bowl of vanilla ice cream down in front of me.

"What's this for? Keeping me quiet? I'm not *seven*, Josh."

He laughs and pours us both a cup of tea.

"So   close shave out there."

"Yeah. Well. I'm fine."

"Stop, look, and listen?" says Josh. "Ring any bells?"

I just scowl at him, arms folded.

"Didn't you have the little 'Cross at the Green' talk in primary school?" he goes on. "That road safety video with the hedgehogs? We did. We had a poster competition. I got summoned to the principal's office because mine was 'too graphic.' Seriously! I thought that was meant to be the point."

Still scowling, I look away.

He tweaks my cheek. "You're trying . . . not . . . to . . . laugh."

"Get off!" But I can't help letting out a half smile. "Look, Josh. This is some kind of lame joke, right? Some . . . *thing* you do to newbies at school to see if they can hack it? Because I'm not impressed."

Josh smiles. "You really think so? After seeing inside the hotel? After what you saw happen on the bus?"

"Okay," I say, "tell me about the bus. How exactly did that happen?"

Josh grins. "Cal's been trying to read it."

"To *read* it?"

"One of her abilities. You'll find all that out soon enough. So, do you want to know what that little test was all about? With the headphones?"

"Yes . . . yes, I do."

"It was a test of mental intuitiveness," he says. "A bit of auto-suggestion, designed to tease out the subconscious. You pulled out very quickly — before you even went fully under."

"And is that good?" I ask cautiously.

Josh presses his fingers together and looks at me intently. "What did you really see?" he asks softly.

I stir my tea. "None of your business. Why do you want to know?"

"Eat up, and I'll tell you. Come on, you *see* things, Miranda. And that test only proves it. You need convincing?"

I was thinking, while he was buying the tea and ice cream, what to say to him. How can I speak to him about the test without mentioning the dream or the Shape? I give it a go.

"Well," I say carefully, "obviously there's *something* weird happening. But . . . I don't believe it *can't* be explained. I mean, you hear these things on the news, don't you? Disappearances, plagues of frogs, and all that. They turn out to have some simple explanation."

Josh sighs, leans back. "There's never been a plague of frogs in Firecroft Bay — well, not yet. Don't believe what you read on the Internet. And don't trust television. *Especially* television."

"My dad used to be on television," I snap at him. I feel myself blushing again. He seems to like making me feel stupid.

"Ah, yes. So he did." Josh doesn't seem surprised or embarrassed. "And what about Mum?"

I concentrate on my ice cream, spearing one of the cream-yellow domes with my spoon. "I don't want to talk about my mother."

"Why not? Tell me, Miranda. . . ."

I look up, suspicious. "What?"

"Does your mum ever say anything? About you . . . sensing things?" He leans forward intently. "You can sense something, can't you?"

I put down my spoon and slump back in the chair. "Sounds like you know all about me, Josh," I say, perhaps a bit too loudly.

People are turning to look at us.

He spreads his hands. "What have I said?"

"Do you *enjoy* this? Power games? Is this why you got me here? Some gullible tween to make fun of?"

"It's not like that," he says calmly.

I push the ice cream away. "All right," I say. "Supposing what you say is true. What happens now?"

I look into his eyes and I realize that something has happened. Since the test, and the near-miss with the truck, and this conversation. I've become a part of his world, and he's a part of mine. And I'm not going to get rid of him, or the others.

Because you know what? I didn't hear or see that truck coming. I walked out in front of it, and right now I should be dead.

But I'm not.

I jumped away in time. And I don't know how I did it.

Josh is right — I can sense something here, right now, that scares me more than anything.

THE BEACH: THURSDAY 17:30

We're walking on the shore near the Esplanade, pebbles going *kssh-kssh* under our feet. The pier's just opened. We can hear the jangle of fairground music and smell the sickly sweetness of cotton candy.

"The test," Josh says. "It showed . . . you're sensitive. You respond. But I think a part of you knows that already."

I'm looking down, poking at the pebbles with one foot, not meeting his gaze. I keep my hands firmly shoved into my jacket pockets, and shrug.

"We need you," he goes on. "You do sense things. And so we think you might be the key to finding out what's really going on in Firecroft Bay, what's causing the increased paranormal activity here." He gently puts a hand on each of my arms, and bobs down so that his blue eyes are level with mine. "Look. Miss Bellini, she . . . well, we all trust her. And she's got an instinct about you."

"She barely knows me," I argue, squirming a little at the way he's holding me.

He smiles. "She's a good judge of character. We all owe her something, Miranda. Me, I was kicked out of a school that was costing my mum and dad an absolute packet, and I washed up here. Fish out of water. But this . . . it gives me a proper purpose. And Cal's mum and stepdad barely know she exists. Their life is running a pub."

"Really?" I'm interested, in spite of myself. "What about Lyssa and Ollie?"

"Little Lyssa — can you imagine how she was picked on at her old school? Mega-brainy and sucks at sports? When she first came she was a timid little thing, hardly dared speak. Look at her now — she's got the confidence of someone twice her age. And Ollie, well, he's got a story or two to tell. I'm sure he will when he knows you better." Josh lets go of me and stands up straight. "Then there's you."

I glance at him, look away. "Sounds like you're saying we're a bunch of misfits."

He grins. "Nobody's a misfit. Some people take longer to find the space they fit into, that's all."

"Doesn't change the fact that you all tricked me into coming to the Seaview."

"Yes. We did. And I'm sorry. But you've got something special, Miranda. You seem to . . . I don't know. . . . You seem to be like a compass. A homing beacon. A . . . a sniffer dog."

"Oh, thanks. Charming."

"Okay. Sniffer dog is bad. Forget I said sniffer dog. I'm sorry. But you're . . . I don't know what word to use. *Intuitive?* But not like Cal. *Psychic*, even? In your own way. I picked up on it that day in the quad. Remember? And we tested it, back there, with the headphones. You want to know how good you are?"

I stare at him. "How good I am at what?"

"Your ability. Your gift."

"I don't have a *gift*."

"Oh, but you do."

"I don't *believe* all that rubbish, Josh. Okay? I don't believe any of it. The whole lot. Mind reading, ghosts, fairies, invisible pink unicorns . . . Give me a break. It's all made up, invented to . . . to stop people from asking questions."

Dark shapes in the night.

Dreams where darkness is alive.

A tune echoing through my mind as I cross the Esplanade.

Something making me get out of the way of a speeding truck.

All made up . . .

"You think?" says Josh, and he looks amused.

"Yes," I say, trying to brazen it out. "It can make people feel better about themselves, make them think the world's more interesting than it really is. But that's about all it's good for. So, if you

50

and your . . . friends back there want to play with your expensive toys, get the Ouija boards out, and go ghost hunting . . . well, you can do it without me."

"Oh, fine," says Josh. "If you want to spend the rest of your life being a Mundane."

"What do you mean, a *Mundane*?"

"You know. Eating cotton candy in amusement arcades. Doing your homework like a good girl. Having nothing more exciting in your life than exams, netball practice, the latest manufactured boy band. That's fine. It's good enough for most of the masses out there. But I think you're better than that. And I think you're denying your true nature. But what do I know?"

"There's nothing wrong with leading a normal life," I say.

"Oh, no. Nothing *wrong* with it."

He is annoying me now. "Get lost, Josh," I mutter, and start to walk away from him.

"Okay," he says. "I will, if you want. *We* will. We'll get lost. We'll leave you alone. If it's what you want."

I stop, turn to face him, and push the hair out of my eyes. I feel an odd sensation in my stomach. An aching, as if I am about to lose something important. It's weird — like nostalgia, only nostalgia for the present. That doesn't make sense.

"Yes," he says. "Me, Ollie, Cal, and Lyssa — we'll just be faces in the corridor, people you pass from time to time and think you ought to know."

I pop seaweed under my boot, pretending not to listen.

51

"And Miss Bellini?" he goes on. "She'll just be a science teacher who drives a beaten-up camper van. And from time to time, you'll hear strange things on the local news, things that make you wonder if you should know more about them maybe, and if you ought to somehow understand them. But you won't belong. You won't know, Miranda. Not *ever*."

I look out to sea, where the waves are swelling and crashing in a constant rhythm behind our conversation. On the distant horizon, a boat cuts through the water, a line of white in the gray-blue. I almost want to be out there right now.

"And now and then," he goes on, "you'll get that sense. The one you already feel. Like there's a realm beyond this one, a secret place behind the curtain of the world. And every so often, you'll be thinking that you *know* things you ought not to. You'll get a feeling, just like you did back there, when you saw that truck coming without even seeing it, and leapt out of the way in time."

"Don't be stupid," I snap back at him, too quickly. "I heard it coming."

"Oh, if you insist. But you know what? I think you knew it was coming. Something you got from the test, maybe . . . something latent that was activated."

I'm confused now. Everything is coming at once. I just want things to be simple.

"Somewhere," Josh goes on urgently, "in some other universe

that just splintered off from this one, you're *dead*. You were hit by that truck and killed. In that other universe, you were never given this chance. If you walk away from us right now, you're saying no to the best thing that's ever happened to you. You're running away from *life*."

He pauses for a second.

"You know, Miranda," he says, "something terrible might be going to happen." He makes it sound like a throwaway remark, but I can't help shivering.

"What?" I ask him. "What's going to happen?"

"Well, that's just it. We don't necessarily know. But you might. And without you, well . . . I suppose we'll just have to figure it out on our own."

I try to let his words sink in. Why am I so important? I'm just Miranda May from London. A few weeks ago, these people didn't know I existed.

"So — bye, then," says Josh. "Have fun."

And he starts to walk away across the beach.

I open my mouth to shout after him. And close it again, shake my head.

Then I shout, *"Wait!"*

Josh stops, turns, with a smile. He's about fifty feet away by now.

"I . . . I do want to know more," I say. "And . . . I want to help. I'm sorry."

Josh strolls back toward me. "Thought you might," he says.

"I don't believe everything you said. But . . . I'm willing to go along with you. For now."

He shrugs. "Your choice," he says, but he's smiling now.

I know it's my choice.

My choice to find out more about why this darkness is haunting me.

CHAPTER SIX

fire

COMPUTER LAB: FRIDAY 11:20

We're all being taught how to use a graphics package called Image-Ination. It's pretty cool, despite the geeky name. You can upload scanned photos of yourself and someone else (we took some last lesson on the digital camera) and it'll morph them into each other. Or it can overlay you into someone else's background and vice versa. You can't see the join — it looks totally real and it gets all the shadows and texture right and everything.

I upload a pic of the JumpJets from their website and flip me and Jade into the pic so that we're onstage with them at the Arena. I look around for Jade to show her what I've done.

"Oh, yeah!" she exclaims.

"Looks so real, doesn't it?" I say. "Amazing!"

And that's when the weird thing happens.

The color of the screen starts to change. The blues and browns and greens, the dull colors, drain away, and the yellows and oranges and reds, all the fiery colors, grow more intense. And it's not just our computer.

"Sir," says Robert Fenwick, the boy sitting next to me, "is it supposed to do that?"

Mr. Heppelwhite leans down and looks at Robert's computer screen. It's gone bright red all over, and a weird whining noise is coming from the speakers.

Mr. Heppelwhite slaps his forehead. "Oh fiddlesticks," he says. "Not *another* virus."

My screen is doing it, too. Turning crimson. New screensaver? Could be, but I doubt it. I look up and down the rows of screens and I see they're all the same. Mine, Robert Fenwick's, Ahmad Hassan's, Jade's, Lyssa's, Ollie's, *everyone's*.

Mr. Heppelwhite is on the phone to the technician. "Bill, can you come down? I think we've got a virus. . . . Well, I don't know what sort! It's making all the computers go insane. The screens are turning red!"

"Orange now, sir," I offer helpfully. My screen is the color of a sunset now, and I swear it's sort of . . . *pulsing*.

"Orange!" says Mr. Heppelwhite into the phone.

"And *hot*," Jade adds, wincing and drawing her hand away from the screen. "Burning hot!"

It's true — the bright orange screen is burning like a five-alarm fire. The whining noise from the speakers is so loud it's hurting my eardrums.

At the same time I'm getting this odd feeling. Kind of like this isn't really happening. Like I did on the bus. There's a thudding in my head. I can smell burning, too. Only it's not burning plastic like you'd expect, but . . . *wood*. Like a blazing fire. My eyelids grow heavy and the room seems to shrink around me so there is just me and my computer in the darkness, the screen glowing, the heat blasting out. And the smell changes to . . . something pungent . . . a chemical. It's making me think about chemistry . . . *Sulfur?* Why can I smell burning sulfur?

"Is it me," I say to Jade, "or are these tables *vibrating?*"

Jade puts her hands flat on the table and her dark eyes widen. "Sir," she calls out, "Miranda's right!"

All the computer screens have now turned a yellowish-white.

Everyone shades their eyes against the brightness.

On the other side of the room, Oliver has jumped to his feet, pushing his chair away from the desk. "Everybody!" he shouts. "Get down! They're going to explode!"

Mr. Heppelwhite rounds on the boy in irritation. "Don't be ridiculous, Ollie."

"But they are!" Ollie yells. "Get on the floor! All of you! Take cover under the tables!"

"Leave it out, Ollie," says Ahmad Hassan, but he cowers under his chair just in case, and several other people duck under the tables and scurry for cover like frightened mice.

Just at that moment, a screen on the far side of the room starts to spark and fizz, and smoke pours out of the sides. Evil-smelling smoke, sharp and sulfurous . . .

Now we all drop to the carpet. And just seconds later, the screen nearest to me explodes in a shower of molten glass. With a *whoomph* and a noise like sizzling sausages. Then the rest of the computers go off like Roman candles. Everyone's screaming.

It's like someone lit a match in a fireworks factory here.

The weird thing is, this all seems sort of familiar. Not déjà vu, no — not like I've experienced it all before. But like . . . this was meant to happen. That it was expected, somehow.

I shake my head. *Get rid of the feeling.*

I see Lyssa under the desk next to me. I wonder if she's scared — paranormal-hunting genius or not, she's only a little kid — and I'm about to hold her hand. But then I realize she doesn't look scared at all. Of course she's not scared. Her face is flushed, her eyes are dancing, and she has her phone out. She's talking in a low, urgent voice over the chaos. To one of the others, no doubt.

It's total madness. Computers are still popping and fizzing all over the room. Glass sizzles as it hits surfaces in molten droplets, leaving a streaming, half-solid mess over the windows, the walls, and the posters. Finally, the noise settles down and it's quiet, apart from a few people sobbing and whimpering.

The room's filled with smoke, but slowly we get the sense that it's safe to put our heads back above the desks again. One by one, we emerge, coughing and looking nervously around.

On the other side of the table from me, Jade picks a piece of keyboard out of her tangled hair. She says something in Italian that I don't understand.

"What was that?" I ask.

"*Epic fail,*" she says with a grin.

Mr. Heppelwhite stands up and clears his throat. "Everyone all right?" he asks nervously. "Nobody hurt?"

It seems nobody is. Although it's pretty clear that nobody's going to be using the lab again for a while. Some of the computers are gaping open, gashed and blackened, the circuitry inside melted into fantastic shapes. Others look black and charred. Only a few have survived intact. Lyssa is up close to one of the charred computers, and, with her handkerchief over her mouth, she's shining a little pen flashlight inside it, looking at the damage.

"Lyssa!" Mr. Heppelwhite snaps. "I wouldn't do that if I were you. Come on! Everyone out, please!"

He takes off one of his shoes and smashes the fire alarm where it says "BREAK GLASS HERE," and then the alarms start echoing through the school.

Bedlam.

Well, cool. This is better than class.

FRIDAY 15:20

The bell jangles. It's a riot, as always on a Friday afternoon.

At the lockers, hordes of kids stream past, gossiping about what happened in the computer lab. I listen to odd snatches.

"I heard it was a *bomb*."

"Don't talk stupid. If it was a bomb, the whole school would have gone up."

"I heard they got attacked by the computers! Fireworks coming out of the screens!"

"Someone said it was a weird kind of virus. They've sealed off the whole section, have you seen?"

Last class of the day — French — has just been a non-starter. I feel sorry for Miss Lowery, because she got nothing much done with us. And at the sound of the bell, everyone pretty much packed up and left before she'd even told us to. We've slammed our lockers shut, and we're stuffing books into our bags for the weekend.

Jade's next to me. She says, "Come round on Saturday afternoon? I've downloaded that bootleg if you wanna listen to it. JumpJets at the London Astoria."

I smile, then glance over her shoulder.

Josh and Cal are standing there, in the corridor, watching me carefully. I meet their gaze and then look back at Jade, who's frowning at me.

"Erm, I dunno," I say. "I'd like to, but . . . I've got a lot going on."

She looks disappointed. "I thought we was mates, Miranda," she says. "I thought you liked me."

I feel bad. I mean, who else was there when I came to Firecroft Bay? Without her, I'd have had nobody else at first. Apart from *them*.

"We are, we are . . . it's just . . ." I'm biting my lip, and now I've given myself away by looking over her shoulder once too often at Josh and Cal.

"Oh, I *see*. I get it. You're hanging out with the Weirdos now."

"They're not weirdos," I say.

"God, you are so lame. I can't believe you've fallen for them. Fancy that Josh Barnes, do you?"

I feel myself turning bright red. "Shut *up*!" I mutter.

She gives me a cynical, sideways smile. "I thought you was different. Thought you could see through all that." She folds her arms. "They're fake, y'know. They're *losers*."

She does the L thing with her thumb and forefinger. But there's something edgy in her expression that tells me she doesn't altogether believe it. Something more than contempt for Josh and the others. Something close to fear.

"This doesn't mean I don't want to be friends with you," I say. "Why do I have to choose?"

Jade's hoisted her bag onto her shoulder. "What-*ever*, Miranda. See you Monday. Maybe."

And before I've had a chance to respond properly, she's headed off, giving Josh and Cal a wide berth. She's out of the door and halfway down the steps, joining the hordes streaming toward the gate.

Josh strolls over.

"She's just a Mundane, Miranda," he says. "Don't lose any sleep over it."

I push him away. "Leave it, Josh."

He backs off, holding his hands up. "Whoah. Sorr-ee. Didn't know you and little Belladonna were such good mates."

I watch Jade going, and then it hits me. Oh, no. She was inviting me to her place for the first time. Where does she live? I don't even know that yet. Maybe it's a big thing to ask people over. She'd told me her mum and dad work from home, running some accounting business. Maybe they're picky about her friends.

And what have I done? I've rejected her.

She's right, isn't she? I'd rather hang out with the Weirdos than go back to a friend's house. How sad is *that*?

"I mean it," murmurs Josh. "Not worth the effort."

"Enough." I glower at him.

And yes, Jade could be right. They *could* be a bunch of nut jobs for all I know. Chasing after stuff that doesn't exist. Like the people who appeared on my dad's old talk show, claiming they'd been abducted by aliens or they'd spotted Elvis working in a burger bar, or they'd seen the Virgin Mary's face in a doughnut. (Sometimes all three, actually. That was a good episode.)

But there is an answer in this, somewhere. An answer I need to find. And something tells me it lies with this shadowy crew. So I am keeping close to them for my reasons — not theirs.

"Tomorrow," says Cal as I walk past her. "Two o'clock. Meet at Craghollow Park. Got a little job for us to do."

And she smiles.

Because she *knows* I'm going to be there.

CRAGHOLLOW PARK: SATURDAY 14:06

Mum's taking Truffle to see our auntie Grace, her older sister, who lives about thirty miles along the coast. It's a bright, sunny Saturday and the sea mist, for now, seems to have been banished.

Mum's happy to drop me off at Craghollow Park because I've said I'm meeting some people from school. I told her their names, but of course they mean nothing to her.

"I'm pleased you've got some friends," she says as we drive along. "I thought it might be difficult. With the move. And . . . everything."

"Yes. It's fine."

"Are they nice? Your friends? Would you like to have one of them round for tea?"

"Round for *tea*?"

"Sorry, sorry." She sighs as the car rounds the corner onto the Esplanade. "Well, you know. Any time you want someone . . . round. To . . . *hang out* or do whatever. It'll be fine."

I roll my eyes.

Beyond the marina, the ring road curves around, heading inland, and there is the metal latticework arch announcing the entrance to the park.

Bit of a spooky name, Craghollow. There's a board beside the entrance — I remember looking at it before — all about its history. It's built on a site where witches were burned in medieval times. Nice.

"Just drop me here, Mum. I'll find my own way."

Though the sun's bright today, it's still chilly, so I'm in my favorite leather jacket and jeans with a woolen scarf. There are a few families out with small kids. Some boys are playing soccer on the grass, and the café's doing good business.

I hurry past the families and the soccer-playing boys. I spot Cal and Lyssa, sitting on the carousel in the play area, slowly spinning round.

Cal's wearing a long white scarf, shades, and a purple velvet coat. She grins when she sees me, and nudges Lyssa. "Told you she'd come," she says, and jumps to her feet. "Right, we're having a girls' day out. And, of course — a little investigation."

For a moment I'm disappointed that Josh isn't here. And surprised at myself. But I don't let it show. I imagine the boys are busy with stuff. Other parts of the investigation, if that's what they want to call it.

"Where are we going?" I ask.

Cal doesn't answer. "Miss Bellini's left me in charge," she says to us both. "So you do as I say, whatever happens, right?"

Lyssa nods eagerly. "Fine by me."

I shrug. "Okay."

We head off toward the edge of the park, passing the fountains and the kids' playground.

"So, do you ever get a day off from this?" I ask, trying to sound more nonchalant than I feel.

"Where's your spirit of adventure, Miranda?" asks Lyssa. I

glance over at her and notice she is playing chess on her phone as we walk along.

"Oh, I've got one, believe me," I answer. "But, you know, girls, *Saturdays*? Aren't Saturdays for chilling? Relaxing? Can't we get the bus to the shopping center, and hang round on the benches, drinking lattes and making fun of other people's ugly shoes?"

"That isn't what we do," says Cal, and the coldness of her response seems to match the expressionless stare of her shaded eyes.

"Okaaaaay," I reply.

Cal turns around, and she looks at me properly for the first time, peering over her shades. "Miranda. This town is full of shadows," she says in a low voice, all sweetness now. "The way I see it, we can spend our lives running *away* from shadows . . . or we can go *toward* them." She smiles. "I know which *I* find more interesting."

We walk on, in silence now.

And before long, I realize where we are heading.

KING EDWARD VI HIGH SCHOOL: SATURDAY 14:15

The gate is brand-new — gleaming, steel mesh, controlled by an electronic lock. We stand there looking up at it.

"School?" I say scathingly. "On the *weekend*?"

Lyssa looks up from her phone chess game. "It's the best time to look around," she says in that unnaturally precise voice. "Nobody's there."

Cal looks up and down the street, checking that nobody is in sight. "Ollie hacked into the network this morning and took care of the security cameras. We don't want the principal asking difficult questions, after all."

"I take it," I say, "that the principal doesn't know what you lot do?"

Cal laughs. "Nobody knows about us," she says. "Officially, our investigations don't exist."

"Except in some underground bunker in the Seaview Hotel?"

Cal nods. "You got it," she says, and flips her phone open. She dials a number. "Now, then . . . we just send the signal. . . ." She clamps her phone over the lock and holds up a finger for silence.

"Breaking and entering?" I say. I try to sound surprised, but I don't quite manage it. Nothing much surprises me about them.

The lock beeps, and there's a click. The gate whirrs and slides back just a few inches — enough for the three of us to squeeze through. When we're inside the playground, Cal sends the signal again and the gate slides shut with a clunk.

Cal grins. "Easy-peasy," she says.

"Lemon-squeezy," I add without thinking, and then I blush as Cal gives me a withering look.

"Grow up, Miranda," she says, then she carries on talking as if I hadn't said anything. "Much harder to do with a padlock, I can tell you."

"New tech's always easier to crack," Lyssa agrees. "Ooh!" she suddenly squeals, looking at her phone.

I jump. "What?"

"The Lucena position!" she exclaims, showing me the screen. "He's lost. *Yessss.*" She looks embarrassed. "Sorry. I get very excited about rook and pawn versus rook endgames."

"C'mon," says Cal, rolling her eyes. "Lyssa, put that away now."

I'm heartened to see that, although Lyssa snaps her phone shut, she sticks her tongue out at Cal first. She may be a paranormal-investigating genius, but she's still nine.

Cal starts striding across the playground toward the main door, like she owns the place. Lyssa skips after her, without a care in the world. I hurry after them, still smarting from Cal's put-down, and nervously looking over my shoulder. I'm convinced the caretaker or even a policeman is going to slap a hand down on my shoulder at any second.

"What are we *doing* here?" I hiss as Cal presses her phone on the front door lock, just as she did with the gates. The doors spring open.

"Going to check out the computer lab," says Lyssa from behind me.

My eyes widen. "It's been sealed off. It's out of bounds!"

Cal stops, folds her arms, and looks down her nose at me. "Miranda," she says, "I know you're new. But come on. You really think anywhere is out of bounds? *Pleeeeease.*"

I ought to be used to Cal's manner by now. I keep having to remind myself she's only a year older than me.

I look at Lyssa, who just shrugs and smiles and follows Cal inside.

What can I do? I follow them into the musty shade of the school. Running toward shadows.

"Do they not have alarms in this place?" I ask.

"Of course they do," says Cal airily, peeking in one classroom after another as we go past. "And they're all linked to one central system. Switching it off is child's play. Luckily, we had a child to do it."

Lyssa licks a finger and dabs an imaginary mark in the air.

"Have you been investigating the virus?" I ask.

Lyssa nods. "Ollie and Josh trawled all the web sources they could find," she says as we hurry along the corridor and up the stairs. "No record of any virus doing that sort of thing to a network. Whatever this is, it's brand-new."

The place seems so weird when it's empty — bigger, darker, more echoing. The chairs, parked on top of the desks, seem to watch over the school like guards. I shudder. School always seems *wrong* when nobody's here.

Up to the second floor. At the end of a long corridor, the computer lab's been sealed off behind clean, shiny white plastic. It makes it look as if the corridor ends in a wall of ice.

"Aren't the police going to be looking round?" I ask nervously.

"The *police*?" says Cal with a snort. "They're out chasing joyriders and beating up student protesters. Er, I mean, keeping the peace. Do you think they're bothered about a computer breakage?"

"Bit more than a breakage, though, wasn't it?" I say.

"Ka-boom!" says Lyssa, and waves her hands in delight.

"Why didn't they all go up?" I wonder out loud. "Some computers were left intact."

"Oh, good question!" says Cal. "Possibly your best so far. Well *done*, Miranda. Asking the right questions can be more interesting than getting the right answers." She rummages in her capacious pockets, then throws me something that I catch instinctively. "Here. You do it."

I realize I'm holding a Swiss Army knife. I look up at Cal, and she nods encouragingly.

I clear my throat, open the knife, and slice a line through the white polyethylene, unsealing the room. I give Cal back her knife, and we step through the gap.

The computer lab's almost completely dark — the only lighting comes from the reddish emergency lights. Someone's put plastic sheeting over all the windows as well, I notice. The computers that exploded are covered with sheeting, too, but the few that weren't damaged are still uncovered.

Cal darts from one computer to another, checking the numbers on the keyboards. "When Ollie hacked the system for us," she says, "he was able to isolate the source of the power surge to a particular subroutine running on one machine. But there was some coding we couldn't get through."

"And I couldn't make sense of everything we did get," Lyssa adds.

"Wow." I tilt my head at Lyssa, mentally unscrambling the geek-speak. "So even Little Miss Sunshine isn't infallible."

Lyssa ignores me. She is checking the back row of PCs. "Here it is," she calls. "Terminal Thirteen. And it's still intact."

"Unlucky for some!" says Cal gleefully. She places her hands on top of the computer and closes her eyes.

"What are you doing?" I ask.

"Trying to read it," she says.

"Read it?" I whisper, baffled.

She nods. "Sometimes objects leave a trace of their user. A memory. Like an imprint. And sometimes, if you have the right kind of mind, it's readable." She shakes her head, looking cross, opens her eyes. "But not today. Lyssa, we'll need to get the data off."

I am curious about this skill of Cal's, but I don't have time to ask anymore. Lyssa nods and sits at the terminal, booting it up.

"Anything you'd like me to *do*?" I ask. "Or am I just here to watch and make admiring comments?"

"Tell you what," says Cal, "you could guard the door if you like."

"So I'm Scrappy-Doo."

"Yeah." Cal grins. "Well, everyone's got to start somewhere."

I hover by the sliced-open plastic, looking and listening down the corridor for any signs of movement.

"What's happening now?" I ask.

Lyssa holds up a stubby red flash drive. "Stealing!" she says.

Lyssa, I have discovered, is a girl of few words. It's left to Cal to give me the proper explanation.

"All we have to do," Cal says, "is rip the event history data off

70

this hard disk and get it back to base for analysis. We can't do that remotely, though. We have to get it off this actual machine. Problem is, a lot of it will be encoded. It's not designed to come off. But if anyone can get through the firewalls, Ollie can."

"Okay, I should say you lost me shortly after *rip*," I admit.

Cal sighs and leans her head to one side. "All right, Scrappy. Just bark if you see anyone coming."

Lyssa plugs the flash drive into the computer's USB port and a number of pop-ups flash up on the screen. I watch in awe as Lyssa's hands flicker across the keyboard, entering strings of numbers.

"Make sure it's not traceable," says Cal. "Can you patch a block in to disguise the incursion?"

Lyssa nods. "Doing it now," she says.

"Couldn't Miss B have done this?" I ask.

Cal shakes her head. "She has to be hands-off sometimes. And her login could be traced." She checks her watch. "Come on, Lyssa. Speed it up."

Lyssa looks up and smiles. "You don't want me to do any damage, do you?" She leans back, hits a couple of keys. "*There.*"

The screen goes black. We all hold our breath.

Across the center of the screen, I can now see a bar, filling up like mercury in a thermometer as the data transfers across.

I blink, remembering the heat when I first saw the computers erupting. I brush the perspiration off my forehead. It's still warm in here.

The bar turns red agonizingly slowly. Beside it, there's a running count in yellow digits of how much data has been transferred to the portable drive: 10%, 15%, 20% . . .

"Don't you find it hot in here?" I ask, a little nervous.

Cal and Lyssa look at each other. Cal looks back at me. "Do you feel something?" she says urgently. She grabs my shoulders. "Don't run away from it. What is it? Tell us."

I shake my head, almost angrily. "No. I don't feel anything."

Something — there — over her shoulder — a fleeting shadow?

I gasp, pull back from Cal. She suddenly scares me.

"You're lying," says Cal.

But then we all hear it. Outside in the corridor, a door slams and the sound echoes through the whole floor. Then there's a jangling noise, and shuffling footsteps.

This is a sound in the real, physical world. And the footsteps are human. I whirl around to face Cal and Lyssa.

"Someone's coming!" I whisper, glancing up the corridor through the gap in the plastic sheeting.

Cal looks at Lyssa. "How much further to go?"

"About fifty percent done," Lyssa says, looking up calmly.

I try to listen, see if I can pick out where the footsteps are coming from, but there's too much echo. I bite my lip, frantically looking back and forth from the corridor, into the room, and out again.

"Seventy percent," says Lyssa from the terminal.

We all hold our breath, uncertain what to do. The footsteps are coming closer.

My heart is thudding. We're going to get caught.

"We need this information," says Cal firmly. "We can't leave without it."

I look in panic at Cal and Lyssa. "Come on! We've got to get out of here — right *now!*"

Outside, the slow footsteps come closer and closer. . . .

CHAPTER SEVEN

data

"THE CLOSET," SAYS CAL. "QUICKLY!"

For a second we stare at her as if she's mad. And then we look over at the big storage closet in the corner of the computer lab, where they keep the manuals and spare parts and all that kind of junk.

"Leave the stick in the machine," says Cal. "We'll have to risk it."

I pull on the handle of the closet door. I pull again. It rattles but it won't budge.

"Locked!" I hiss at Cal.

She flips out her Swiss Army knife again, slides it in between the door and the frame, and levers expertly. With a judder and a creak, the door snaps open.

"In!" she says to me and Lyssa, bundling us inside.

We pile in, squat down on the bottom shelf underneath all the stuff. Cal pulls the door behind us and holds it shut. The enclosed space smells of metal and paper. Cal's on one side, Lyssa and I are on the other. And we hold our breath. I try to peep out through the crack, but Cal waves a finger at me and shakes her head.

I want to see what's making that noise. Human intruders I can deal with. But I'm worried about what else I sensed back there, just for a moment.

There was a shadow.

And now someone steps into the computer room. We hear the footsteps stop, and we hear a *tut-tut* sound.

"Bloomin' vandals," says a gravelly voice.

We look at each other, because we all recognize the voice. It's Mr. Harbinson, the school custodian. I almost sigh out loud with relief. I imagine he is looking at my clean incision in the plastic across the door, and I feel a twinge of guilt.

"Blimey," he says. "I dunno."

He's still muttering to himself. His footsteps come closer to the closet. We hardly dare breathe. We hear him bending down, then we hear something shuffling on one of the desks. I realize straight-away what has happened — he's found the computer on, and he's moving the mouse around to see if anything appears.

A second later, the whine of the computer cuts out — Mr. Harbinson has switched it off, muttering, "Gawd, I dunno," again.

I cross my fingers. I hardly dare look at Lyssa or Cal.

Now, at last, his footsteps start to go away again, and we hear him wheezing and coughing as he shuffles out of the computer lab.

He'll be on the phone to the principal, I imagine, to report that someone has been messing about in the computer lab. I hope we'll be miles away by then. But we still have to get out of here.

Cal nods and points to me. I carefully open the closet door a crack and check the coast is clear before emerging, trying not to make any sound. Lyssa rushes over to the computer, which is now switched off.

But the flash drive has been left in the machine. Lyssa grins at me and Cal before pulling it out and pocketing it.

"Lucky!" I mouth.

Old Harbinson can't have spotted anything other than the fact that the computer was left on. With any luck, what was displayed on the screen wasn't of any interest to him.

"I just hope we got all the data before he cut the power," Cal whispers.

I check at the doorway.

"All clear!" I hiss.

We tiptoe our way back along the corridor. We can hear Harbinson whistling downstairs, clanking about and doing something in his little room off the main downstairs corridor.

"Back to the main entrance," whispers Cal. "Quick!"

Less than half a minute later, we are back in the lobby, and Cal has her phone out again. I look nervously over my shoulder, but Harbinson's whistling is still echoing through the school, giving us a good idea of where he is.

Cal thumbs the number for whatever signal it is she uses, and the electronic lock springs open.

We're out, racing down the playground toward the gate, and we have our treasure.

THE SEAVIEW HOTEL: SATURDAY 16:32

Miss Bellini looks across the big wooden table at each of us in turn.

"All right," she says. "So what do we know? Let's ask our newest member. Miranda?"

We're in a transparent pod that serves as Miss Bellini's office — it's held by girders right up in the ceiling, and is accessible only by a ladder.

Everyone is looking at me. Miss Bellini with her warm, dark eyes peering over her metallic glasses. Josh, sprawling on a chair, one arm over the back of it. *Where's he been?* I wonder. Cal, lean and graceful. Lyssa, hands folded on the desk as if she's in school. And Ollie, his face alert and keen beneath his mop of white-blond hair. There's a laptop computer open on the table.

I'm surprised how quickly I've been accepted here. How easily I seem to fit in.

"Well," I say carefully, "I think we're dealing with something that, for some reason, needs *energy*. The bus — practically all the heat energy was extracted from it, right? Every ounce."

"Joule," says Josh.

"What?" I say, irritated.

"You measure energy in joules, May. Not grams. Don't you learn *anything* in your science class?"

Miss Bellini holds up a hand. "Go on, Miranda," she says.

77

I try to focus. I've been thinking about this. "The engine seized up, the gasoline froze —"

"Diesel," interrupts Josh.

I look at him irritably. "All right, the *diesel* froze . . . the metal and plastic started icing up. I think that was a *massive* exchange of energy going on. As if some kind of reaction was happening that needed a lot of power. And then again, with that virus in the computer lab — something was channeling an awful lot of electrical energy through that one computer, Terminal Thirteen, which turned into heat and blew the whole system."

Josh gives a low whistle. "Not bad. Not bad at all!"

"What's the freezing point of diesel?" asks Ollie.

"Good question," says Miss Bellini. "The thing about petroleum-derived diesel is that it's not just *one* chemical. It's a mixture of different sorts of hydrocarbons. In Alaska, trucks can still run in temperatures of minus 46 Celsius. I'd say anywhere between, ooh . . . about minus 70 and minus 185 degrees Celsius."

"That's pretty freakin' cold," says Josh. "What have we got on the computer data?"

"All extracted," replies Ollie, and spins the laptop around so we can all see it. The screen shows a timeline graph — a wobbly green line against a black background, plotting network activity against time. "A viral spike was inserted into the network's copy of the Image-Ination software at 11:02, *here*. It attacked the system from within. Now, the thing about *most* computer viruses is that they're a pain, they can wipe your data off, but they don't actually damage the hardware itself. Well, this one did."

"How?" I ask, genuinely interested.

"Yes, how?" echoes Cal. "A computer virus causing an overload of electrical energy? It doesn't make sense."

Ollie grins. "I was hoping you'd ask. The virus didn't come from Terminal Thirteen, but for some reason that was the first one to be zapped."

Lyssa says, "The Image-Ination software's not corrupted, is it? No, so the virus is a decoy. It was *inserted* there so that when the techies came along to find out what went wrong, they'd be led up the garden path."

"So," says Miss Bellini softly, taking her glasses off and twirling them between thumb and forefinger, "our conclusion is . . . ?"

Ollie says, "The overload was caused by something *outside*. Something, or someone, in the room."

There is a moment's silence, and we all draw breath and look at one another.

Then Cal says cautiously, "Something . . . transferring energy straight into the computer network?"

"Or drawing it out," I suggest.

Everyone turns to look at me.

God, I hate it when they do that. But I have got something to say, and it seems they're listening.

"Go on," says Miss Bellini.

"Well, that can cause a power surge, too, can't it? And it would make more sense. This . . . whatever it is we're fighting, it must need energy."

Josh hasn't spoken much yet, but now he unfurls himself from his chair and leans forward. "What about," he says, "some bizarre form of energy that can adapt itself to its surroundings? Like a chameleon?"

"Very good, Joshua," says Cal. "You're *thinking*. Is it your birthday?"

Josh smiles at her. "Just to please you."

Cal smiles back, and the two of them hold their gaze just long enough for me to see the special look of understanding that passes between them. They seem close, Josh and Cal. They bicker and banter, but I can tell there's something there. Oh yes, even I can see that. And why does this bother me? It shouldn't.

"I'll start looking some things up," says Ollie, gathering his notes together. "Got a lot to go on."

"And I'll take a closer look at the data from the computer with you," says Lyssa with her usual eagerness. "Something else may come up. Something I missed."

Miss Bellini smiles, leans back in her chair, spreads her hands. "This is what I like to see, folks. Self-motivation. Now, Miranda."

"Yes, Miss Bellini?" My voice sounds thin.

She smiles. "Good work. Go back home for now. You look tired. But come back on Tuesday after school. I have something to show you."

THE OLD VICARAGE: SUNDAY 14:37

I'm lying on my bed. My eyes are so heavy. I don't feel too well. I think I need to sleep. What is the matter with me? Glandular fever? Flu? Feels weirder than that, like the times when I've been sort of disconnected from reality — on the freezing bus, seeing the Shape, that shadow in the computer lab. There's an odd weakness in my body and bones.

Mum's "helper" Tash has taken Truffle for a walk, while Mum's house visiting. Outside, the spring sunlight is struggling through low gray clouds.

I don't know if my eyes are open or closed.

I think I'm down on the Esplanade. It is dusk, and the place is deserted. This is so strange. Am I awake? I hear screeching seagulls and I imagine . . . dream . . . no, more than that, I *feel* I'm barreling along the seafront with the cold salt wind in my face. I can smell that seaweedy death-smell again, that odor of burning. *Sulfur.* I stop, shade my eyes against the setting sun.

And there.

It's standing at the waterline again. Just as it was that day, before I ate ice cream in the café with Josh.

But this time it's a recognizable Shape. Human. It's wearing a long, dark dress, and its face is shrouded by a hood. A girl . . . ? And she's beckoning to me. I am shaking with fear. I can hear my own ragged breath, feel my heart pumping away.

Am I waking or sleeping?

*   *   *

The room stabilizes around me. I am awake now.

I take several deep breaths, feeling my mouth dry and claggy with fear. I look around the room. Nobody but me, all my usual clutter, my clothes and posters.

But my heart is still pounding.

I need to get away from the bed. I need to get out of the bedroom. This bed and this bedroom, they're where I first saw the Shape, where the terror started. I can't let this happen anymore.

Do not dream.

And yet . . . I need answers.

I remember what Cal said that day in the park. *Running away from shadows or toward them? I know which I find more interesting.*

Still shaking, I go downstairs and pour a Cola-Maxx, shove my iPod into the dock on the counter, and flick through the tracks.

Nothing matches my mood. I don't want the Janies, Crank, or Elusive today. Not even the JumpJets. I need something empty and meaningless. I flick down further and there are some dance tracks one of the boys from my old school bootlegged for me. MC Gaia and the Force. Means nothing. Don't think I've ever listened to it.

I put it on while I slurp my drink. It's good. Pounding and rhythmic, but kind of lush, echoing through the kitchen with a bass line as strong and head-kicking as the cola, with a lilting keyboard line like froth over the top. Good Sunday afternoon old-school techno. *"And if you know that I love you, you'll feel it in the air, feel it everywhere . . ."* Stupid lyrics, but I'm nodding along to the track, leafing through a local paper Mum has left lying on the table. I'm trying to tell myself I feel normal, but I'm still shaking from the dream. I try to take an interest. Stuff about gardening shows, local children getting awards, something about the new power station going online . . .

"And if you know that I love you, you'll feel it in the air, feel it in the air —"

The sound skips for a second. I wonder if it is supposed to do that. It skips again, missing several beats.

I go over to my iPod to see what's wrong with it. The music's not only skipping now but trapped in a two-second loop.

"Feel it in the — feel it in the —"

And then it stops, goes silent.

I frown. The screen's still lit up. It looks as if it should be working. Something else comes through the speakers.

Whistling.

A pure, clear tune, in an open, echoing space. I couldn't place it when I first heard it on the headphones in the Seaview Hotel. But now I recognize it. An old nursery rhyme tune from deep in the past.

Ring around the rosie, a pocket full of posies . . .

I tear the iPod out of the dock and hurl it across the room. It smacks against the tiles, skids, and comes to rest. Just to make sure, I unplug the dock as well.

I am shaking, sweating, breathing hard.

I'm not dreaming. Just like the time on the Esplanade when I saw the Shape. I'm awake. Something is happening to me, invading my life, and I can't seem to do a thing about it.

KING EDWARD VI HIGH SCHOOL: MONDAY 12:32

I'm in the library, trying to look stuff up for my Geography project, and something's thumped down on the table in front of me — a big blue box file.

"You've blotted my ink," I point out, looking up at Josh.

"Who cares about that?" Josh says. He pulls my book out from under the file and glances at it. "*Chalk Escarpments of the South Downs.* God, how dull. Is that what twelve-year-olds study in Geography these days?"

"Joshua Barnes!" hisses the librarian, Miss Challis, glowering at him from her desk. "If you have a class to go to, please get there. If not, please be quiet! People come here to work!"

"Sorry, miss. Just going, miss." Josh grabs my arm. "Come on."

I'm gathering up my stuff, frantically stuffing it into my bag. "I've got netball next."

"Nope. You just got lucky. Note from your mum," he says, texting with one hand as he shoves me out of the library doors.

"I did?" I ask.

"Miss B will sort it out."

"Josh, Miss B can't *forge* notes from my mum."

"You'd be surprised." He grins, waits for some stragglers to hurry past to their classes, then holds up the box file. "Well? Aren't you going to ask me what this is all about?"

I shrug. "What's . . . this all about?"

"Thought you'd never ask. Here!"

I realize just in time that he's going to throw me the file, and I catch it, gasping at the weight of it.

"Good stuff, Miranda," he says. "Come with me."

I don't immediately follow him.

"Miranda?" he says, doing a comical wave in my face. "All okay?"

"Um, yeah, yeah." I shake my head. "I'm fine. I just . . . didn't sleep very well last night. I've been . . . drinking Cola-Maxx."

"Oooh, careful with that," Josh says. "Strong stuff, you know. Can get you hooked."

"Can it?" I say in alarm.

"No! Are you okay, Miranda? Really?"

I nod hastily. "Really. Fine. Where are we going?"

It turns out we're going to the Physics lab, where there's a free computer. The technician glares at us but Josh just tells him we are doing some work for Miss Bellini. He trudges off. I bet he's going to check, and I bet we'll turn out to have a backstage pass from Miss B.

Okay, so I'm starting to enjoy this. It makes me feel like I can get away with all sorts of stuff.

I open the box file. It's dusty and full of old floppy disks, those big square things that people stopped using, like, *decades* ago.

"We'll never be able to read these!" I say.

"Oh, you think?" Josh taps something at the side of the

computer — a cream-colored disk drive with a thin, wide slot, attached to the main machine by a wide strip of colored wires. "Miss B saved this from the scrap heap over the summer. A wise move."

"What is all this, anyway?" I ask, handing Josh the first disk in the pile.

"Records of unsolved phenomena, going back thirty years. Ollie got it all for me. Data we always meant to get transferred onto something more up-to-date, but never did. But it means it's not exactly easy to access." He slots the disk in and the drive chugs and whirrs like a food mixer. "Blimey, these old things make a racket."

"What are we looking for?"

"Anything to do with unexplained power surges. Energy exchange. That kind of thing."

"We've got to go through the whole lot?" I say in horror, looking at the endless lines of old-fashioned, pixelly white text scrolling on the black screen.

Josh claps me on the shoulder. "No, not 'we.' *You* do."

"What?" I look up.

He slings his bag over his shoulder. "Rugby practice," he says with an apologetic grin. "And I don't have a note."

"Why can't you do this?" I ask with a scowl.

"Cal asked me to get you to do it."

"Oh, I see. And lover-boy *always* does what Cal says."

He rolls his eyes theatrically. "It's not like that."

"Isn't it?" I ask with an impish smile. "If you say so, Josh."

He opens the stockroom door and pauses on the threshold. "Think of it as earning your stripes. Efficiency is ninety percent delegation, you know."

And he's gone.

I hate this. I really *hate* it.

And Josh? He is *enjoying* it.

I sigh, looking at the pile of old disk records again.

I'm not stupid. There's no way I'm looking through all this stuff on my own without any idea of what it might mean. So I do what any sensible person would do. I may not be an IT expert, but I can do this. I slot the disks in one by one, copy all the data onto a document, put it in my secure web space, and reboot.

Just as I'm slipping out of the deserted Physics lab my phone burbles at me.

It's a text from Jade.

WHERE R U BABE? NEED 2 SPK

I text her back, hurrying along the corridor:

2 BUSY NOW MEET @ BRK

I'm glad for the opportunity to chat. Jade and I have unfinished business.

* * *

At break time, I spot Jade instantly. She's hopping up and down on the far side of the playground.

"You're in deep, babe," she says to me, narrowing her eyes.

"Miss Venderman wanted to know where you was in PE. I had to cover for you. Said you'd been sick in the toilets and gone to the nurse's office."

"Thanks," I say. (*So much for the note from my mum, Josh,* I think bitterly.)

"Don't mention it," she says, looking away. She offers me a licorice twist, which I take gratefully. The sharp taste reminds me I haven't had one for months. "So where was you?" she says.

"Don't tell me. The netball team fell apart without me?"

Jade gives me one of her sudden, warm grins. "Well, not really. Did you blow it off? Respect. Wish I could've." She stares at me. "You *did*, didn't you? You cheeky cow, you blew it off! It's to do with the Weirdos, innit?"

"What did you want to tell me?" I ask, avoiding the question.

Jade glances around. There's a few older boys smoking in a huddle, and in the other direction a crowd of girls trading Zillah Zim cards. Some kids from our class are giggling and gossiping on the wall. She grabs my arm and pulls me around behind the garbage bins.

"Ow!" I rub my elbow.

"Sorry. It's just . . ." Jade looks down at the playground, as if unsure quite how to speak to me.

"Look, my telepathy isn't very advanced," I say. "You're going to have to use your voice."

She looks up, openmouthed.

"That was a *joke*, Jade. So come on. Out with it."

She bites her lip, peers around the bins one more time to check we are not being listened to. "I'm worried about you," she says.

"About me? Really?"

"You don't look well," she says. "You taken a look at yourself, recent-like?"

I run a hand through my hair. "I feel fine, Jade. Really, I do."

Jade flips a mirror out of her pocket and holds it in front of my face. I look at my wobbling reflection. I suppose I do look a bit gray, and my eyes are sleepy hollows. My hair is hanging down in limp strands, too.

"Somethin's botherin' you, ain't it?" Jade asks. "Somethin' big. I bet it's to do with them."

"Them?"

"Yeah. Them Weirdos." Jade lifts her hands and makes her fingers into claws. "You've not been the same since you started hanging round with them."

"I'm really fine, okay?"

She scowls. "If you're sure. It's just that . . . you don't seem to have much time for your *normal* mates anymore."

"Look," I say, "let's talk after school." I hesitate. "Maybe at your place . . . ?"

Jade's smile vanishes. "That wouldn't be cool."

"Oh. Sorry . . . I just thought —"

She shakes her head firmly. "Me mum and dad, they . . .

well, they, like I said, they work at home. Don't like me bringing friends back."

"Right," I say uncertainly. "Okay."

That's a bit different from the other day, then. What's changed?

The bell jangles, and we have to go back inside.

CHAPTER EIGHT

tricks

HOUSEMAN BOULEVARD: MONDAY 15:37

I'm following Jade home. I don't like what I'm doing, but I have to make her realize I *do* still want to be her friend, only it's complicated. But I also want to know why she didn't invite me back to her house. What's going on?

Keeping her in sight, I hurry along Houseman Boulevard, the two-lane highway near the sea. There's Craghollow Park on one side, and hotels and nice houses lining the other. It's got wide walkways bordered by neat grass shoulders.

Jade is up ahead on the curve of the road, just where it heads down into town. I'm not going to catch up to her in time to see which way she goes.

I pick up my pace, and close the gap between us to a few hundred yards. And then I see her swing right at the statue of Queen Victoria, cutting into the park entrance under the canopy of chestnut trees. She's heading across Craghollow Park, striding quickly toward the exit on the far side that leads to the Millennium Estate, and now I've got this idea in the back of my head, one that I think is going to turn out to be right.

As I leave the park, I'm just in time to see Jade turn down into the tree-shaded boulevard of Shelley Drive. My instinct is looking good.

I hurry to the corner by the street sign and watch from the shadow of the hedge.

Jade gets her key out. She's going up the long drive of a big, redbrick, turreted building that dominates this side of the road. I watch her go up the steps to the front door, put her key in the lock, and go inside.

So I was right.

I didn't know.

But now she's going to think I did — that I didn't believe what she said about her mum and dad — and that was why I didn't want to come home with her. Because she lives *there*, in the Copper Beeches Children's Home.

THE OLD VICARAGE: MONDAY 22:22

All the twos. The time gleams on my silver watch, beside the bed, as I try to drift into sleep. The coast is never still, not even at night. I can hear the sea washing the bay, shouts carried on the wind from the harbor, even a distant throbbing boom, which is probably the late-night ferry to Brittany.

I close my eyes and think of the boat, a little glittering city on the water, leaving the harbor, keeping between the flashing lights that mark the safe route and heading out into the cold, blue-black darkness beyond.

I close my eyes, and the deep, rushing sound is now something else entirely: *the intense roaring of a fire.*

I am standing at the edge of a field, and the slim figure of a girl is running toward me in slow motion. Behind her, an entire forest is on fire, a wall of flame, the smoke billowing into the clear sky. I try to focus, my eyes feeling heavy and crunchy.

The girl skids to a halt, staring at me with big eyes from a smoke-blackened face, her coal-black hair wild and singed. She shakes her head silently and turns as if to run away from me.

"Stop!" I call, or try to. I have no idea if the words come out, or if they're torn away by the smoky wind. "Come back! Tell me who you are."

She stops, looking over her shoulder. As I approach her, I feel a sense of dread. Why? Surely she's only a girl, like me. She turns away from me. I can see my own hand reaching out toward her. Nearer, nearer, and nearer still. I am almost touching her shoulder.

And then she turns back toward me.

Now, framed by the wild black hair, is an ancient, yellow-skinned face, and it is covered with thick, dark pustules. She opens her mouth, showing stumps of brown teeth, and hisses.

The shock kicks all the breath from me.

• • •

I lie awake in my bed, counting, breathing, letting myself focus on the details of my room. The square of light that is my window slowly tunes itself in. I turn, look at my watch. 22:35. Still dark, the sea still breathing deeply.

I turn over, eyes wide open, staring at the wall.

All I want is a quiet life in my new town with Mum and Truffle, trying to forget that Dad's never going to hug me again, dance with me, pick me up and rub his bristly chin against my cheek the way he used to. To forget that I've been torn apart.

I can't do this on my own anymore.

I have to let *them* help.

SEAVIEW HOTEL: TUESDAY 16:17

I'm with Ollie at one of the computer desks. He's been working through all the data I transferred off the old floppy disks. Lyssa's doing something up on one of the little platforms. Sounds like she's sorting out piles of old books.

Over on the other side of the Datacore, as they call it, Josh and Cal are playing pool again. It's a game that seems to involve a lot of giggling and hair tossing (her), and a lot of cracking of bad jokes and posing with the cue (him).

I'm half watching them. He's helping her line up a shot, and that involves getting behind her, up close, placing his hands on hers.

It's time to ask for help, and it occurs to me that I'd rather ask Ollie than the others.

"What do you know about 'Ring Around the Rosie'?" I ask him.

As usual, Ollie doesn't seem at all surprised to be asked random questions. "It's a rhyme," he says. "About the Black Death, apparently."

"The Black Death?"

"There's no proof or anything, and people claim it's all made up, but yeah, it's supposedly about the Black Death. Also known as the Bubonic Plague. From the Middle Ages. The ring is the rash that people broke out in, the posies of flowers were to ward off the Plague, and the *ashes, ashes* bit is the, well, dropping down dead." He shrugs. "There's not meant to be anything to it, though. No evidence there ever was."

"Right."

"Something you want to share?"

I shiver, thinking about my dream. About the burning forest and the hissing Shape, the dark-haired girl with yellow, pustuled skin. And all the other things in my head. The burning smell, the sea fog, the heat of fire.

"It's just that . . . recently . . . I've been . . . hearing it."

"Yeah? Hearing it how?"

I hesitate. "I'm not quite sure I understand what I'm going through here, Ollie. I don't think anyone can explain it to me."

He pauses, then simply nods. "Okay. Oh, Miss Bellini wants to see you, when you're ready."

I'm grateful for his tact. I glance at the giggling pool players, and head up the metal ladder to the Pod.

I find Miss Bellini looking down at the sprawling technology below.

"How much *did* this all cost?" I ask curiously. Then, in case that sounds rude, I go on, "If you don't mind my asking."

Miss Bellini chuckles. She doesn't seem offended. "Very little, at first. And various legal quirks have been used to make sure the place isn't developed. After all, it suits our purposes to keep it as a ruin."

I nod. I can see that. "And all this gear?"

"There are . . . benefactors," says Miss Bellini enigmatically. "People sympathetic to our cause, who don't wish to become directly involved. But we put a lot of it together ourselves."

"But what's it all about, really? I mean, how did it *start?*"

She bends toward me, her eyes full of some inner light. "This battle against darkness has been going on for a long, long time in some form. For centuries."

"And how do you fit in, Miss B? How did you end up here, a teacher in a dead-end town and running this weird . . . setup?"

Okay. So I'm feeling bold. But she isn't really answering my questions.

"You know," she says carefully, "we are still fighting a war, Miranda. It may not look like a war to you, and this is only one small, insignificant corner of it, but a war it is. Against forces that want to drag this world into their darkness. Each time, the enemy has a different name, a different face. But you come to recognize it. A child with a gift like yours, especially so. Psychic, intuitive powers are a major weapon in the fight against the darkness."

I wrinkle my nose. "You really think I have a gift?"

"Oh, yes," she says, and she sounds perfectly serious. "You see things. You know things. For you, it will be confusing at first. A mixture of messages and sensations. Like everything coming through at once. Like you can't tell, sometimes, if you've had a dream, a daydream, or a psychic experience. Am I right?"

I nod.

She looks sympathetic. "That will pass. You'll come to understand it better. To control it, even. And of course, my dear, there may be more you can do. We're still learning about you, after all."

"But it was just luck that I ran into you all, wasn't it? I mean, just coincidence?"

Miss Bellini smiles. "Things are rarely *just* coincidence, Miranda. A network of invisible threads binds this universe together."

I'm thinking about my experiences at home. The darkness of my dreams invading the real world, and the song on my iPod that should not have been there. The girl and the burning forest. The Shape.

I tell Miss Bellini about the strange rhyme, and how I thought I recognized it. I haven't told her everything yet, about the dreams and so on, but I want to keep something back for myself until I am absolutely sure I can trust everyone.

"Ollie says it's from the time of the Black Death," I say.

Miss Bellini nods. She doesn't seem surprised. "Set one thread vibrating," she says, "and you cause others to shake, and others still, until, somewhere in the web, something snaps, something breaks. And before you know it, the world is out of kilter. And someone has to watch for these vibrations, and know them, and find what causes them. That's us." She pauses, as if taking in what I have told her. "Thank you for telling me, Miranda. Now, come here. I'm going to show you how much you know without even realizing it."

She pulls on a pair of gloves and beckons me over to her desk. She takes a small silver box out of the drawer. She opens it, and inside there is a little white ball, like a Ping-Pong ball, only smaller. She holds it up between her gloved thumb and forefinger, and places it on the desk. It doesn't look like plastic — it's so white and smooth it could be made of marble, or even ice. Beside it, she places three silver cups, the size of grapefruit halves.

"Just a game," Miss Bellini says. "An old friend from a fair in New Orleans gave it to me. Look." And she puts the ball under one of the cups, and slowly starts to move them around the table. After a few seconds, she stops moving them. "Which one?" she says with a smile.

I don't hesitate. I've been keeping my eye on it all the time. "That one," I say, indicating the half sphere in the middle.

"Very good," says Miss Bellini, and lifts up the hemisphere to show me I am right. "Now — again, only *faster*."

This time, her hands flash across the table more quickly, and although I'm trying my hardest to concentrate and keep my eye on the cup I *know* the ball is under, it's just not possible. So when Miss Bellini finishes moving them around, and gestures for me to pick, I know — and I think she knows — that I'm just guessing.

I point to the one on the left. "That one."

Miss Bellini sighs. "Oh, bad luck." She lifts the hemisphere to show it's empty, then shows me the ball under the right-hand one. "The speed of the hand, Miranda May, deceives the eye. *But . . .*" She holds up a finger, smiling in that strange way of hers that makes her eyes crease. "Do it again. Don't look. Just think. *See* the ball in your mind. Now."

Miss Bellini moves the cups on the desk, slowly at first, and then with increasing speed. I try to do what she asked. Her hands move faster and faster. I think. I think. *I think.* Then she stops.

I don't know why, and it seems totally random, but something is screaming a word inside my head.

"Left," I say. "Left!"

Miss Bellini lifts the left-hand cup.

The ball is under it.

I'm astonished, but I try not to show it. I shake my head, gripping the table. "I could . . . just be lucky," I say.

"Of course. Very likely. You have a one-in-three chance of getting the right answer by pure luck, as does anyone." Miss Bellini's voice is soft and warm. In class, I've noticed that she uses the same voice whether she is praising you or telling you off, so you're never *quite* sure where you are with her. I think this is part of why her pupils respect her. "So, let's try again," she says. "Go."

The cups move, clicking and swishing, and after a few seconds Miss Bellini tells me to guess.

This time, that feeling tells me to go for the one in the center. I point to it. Miss Bellini lifts it up and I'm right.

I am startled now, my stomach churning with that mixture of

excitement and anxiety you get on the first day of school.

Miss Bellini does the trick again and again. Each time, I *think* myself into finding the right answer rather than trying to look for it. Most times, I get it right. I'm only wrong once out of about ten turns.

"Surprised?" says Miss Bellini as she hides the ball under a cup again.

I nod instinctively, then straightaway I wonder if I should be surprised at all. After everything that's happened, I should almost have expected it.

"Well, it's quite natural in a girl of your age and ability. *Over there!*" snaps Miss Bellini suddenly, pointing — and I look, startled, out of the glass wall of the Pod. I can't see anything unusual. "Now tell me," she says, gesturing to the table. "Tell me which one. Tell me now!"

"Ummm . . ." I know I've lost the sense. I point to the one on the right anyway.

Miss Bellini sighs and lifts it up It's empty.

"Always be alert to distractions," she says, lifting the middle hemisphere. It's also empty. And now she lifts the one on the left — to show that there is no ball under there either.

I gawk.

"Expect the unexpected," says Miss Bellini with a smile.

"It can't have just gone. Where did it go?"

"You may well ask." Miss Bellini smiles, and taps her nose.

"Come back when you have an answer, Miranda. A *scientific* answer, if you please."

I climb back down the ladder. When I reach the bottom I look up to the Pod. Miss Bellini is standing at the window. She has her hands on the glass and her head down, as if she is deep in thought. Either that, or terribly sad about something.

CHAPTER NINE

friends

THE OLD VICARAGE: WEDNESDAY 00:05

I still can't sleep. But at least it means I'm not dreaming. It's really warm for the time of year and I'm lying there with just a sheet on, turning things over in my mind.

Miss Bellini has told me to expect the unexpected. That's usually one of those things adults say when they're not really sure themselves what they mean. But Miss Bellini means it, and she knows what she means, too.

I can hear Truffle snuffling and gurgling in his room down the landing. He's going to wake up any minute now, I know it. When I went to bed there was still a light under Mum's office door. I know not to disturb her when she's working late.

Who am I? Where am I going? Before all this, I'd have thought: Is this it, then? Do I just have to plod on through school, exams, university? Get a boyfriend, get married, get a job, get a house, go to work until I *die*?

But now there's something new.

Something exciting. Something different.

But I'm still lying here, afraid to sleep again. Afraid that the dream and the Shape may come again . . .

Truffle's snuffles have turned to wails. I can hear someone whistling in the street outside. A drunk coming back from the pub, I expect. I think I vaguely know the tune, but I can't place it.

Truffle has started to do that desperate hiccuppy crying now. I wonder what does *his* head in? I feel pretty envious of him. I mean, what a life. Eat, poo, sleep. I've seen pictures and videos of me as a baby, and I can't believe I used to be like that, too.

But I like to watch the videos, because my dad is on them.

Some days, I almost forget what his voice used to sound like, even though I remember the words he spoke. *Hey, Panda. Give us a hug.* How warm his eyes were. How he —

Hang on. That whistler outside in the street.

My entire body goes prickly and rigid as the random notes begin to form a tune.

Ring. Around. The Rosie.

It's colder now. I sit up, pull the covers toward me in a sudden, protective movement, as if I have sensed it, felt it before I actually see it.

Like I knew about the truck on the Esplanade.

A Pocket. Full. Of Posies.

And then I see it.

Just a dark flash, reflected in the mirror of my wardrobe. A long, shimmering stripe of darkness, a hint of a face. The whistling is louder. It's not outside.

It's in my head.

It's in my room.

The Shape is in here with me.

For a moment, I'm unable to move, weak and shaking. The room swims in front of me and turns dark. There is a swirl of sounds and images around and inside my head: screeching seagulls, sea fog, clanging bells, fire crackling, forests burning, the swishing of an endless bleak sea. The drumming of horses' hooves. The ravaged face of the girl.

I feel a chill, as if the sea fog has reached into the house and taken hold of me, stealing into my nose and mouth. I try to open my mouth and scream, but I can't.

I scrabble about for something that's real. My bedside table, my watch — no, not that. My alarm clock. I pick up the clock and hurl it at the intruder. The clock arcs across the room and smashes against the wardrobe mirror.

I'm back. Gasping for breath.

My door thumps open. Light floods the room. Mum's there, looking frantic, her hair a mess and her glasses pushed up onto her forehead.

I can see myself in the mirror. I'm shuddering, sitting right in the corner of my room with the duvet pulled up tight. Across the landing, Truffle is screaming now, even louder than I did. I blink against the light and feel myself go cold with sweat.

"Miranda," Mum says, "whatever is the matter?"

There's only me and her in the room. I can see that now.

"Nightmare, Mum," I croak. "Just a bad dream."

"Oh, sweetie." She's there beside me, stroking my hair and kissing my cheek. "It's not real. Just put it out of your mind."

I'm trembling, and even though I can feel Mum's comforting arms around me, they don't keep out this terrifying new world.

She pulls back, looking at me, taking my face in her hands. "You look so tired. Are you working too hard at school?"

I shake my head. "No. Really, I'm not. Just . . . I think I've got a bit of a cold."

"Honey and hot lemon," says Mum calmly. "These spring colds can sneak up on you. I'll go and make you some."

COPPER BEECHES: WEDNESDAY 16:07

After school, I make a decision. I'm going to do something to make me forget about dreams and shapes. Something normal. And I need to do it, anyway.

I walk along the road by the park and easily find the big redbrick house again. I knock at the door, and a red-faced woman answers, wiping her hands on her apron. "Hello, love," she says, raising her eyebrows.

"Um, I've come to see Jade," I say nervously.

"Oh, have you, now?" She folds her arms and looks me up and down. "Well, you seem like a nice girl. Maybe you'll help her settle down a bit." She ushers me in. "I'm Mrs. Armitage. Probably told you all sorts about me, hasn't she?"

I smile nervously, not wanting to say that Jade and I actually haven't talked about this place at all, because I don't officially know that she lives here.

"Settle down?" I repeat as I step into the hall.

Mrs. Armitage taps her nose. "Bit of a wild child, our Jade."

I grin. "Yeah, I know."

"She's in the back somewhere, I think."

"Thanks," I say.

I'm being normal today. Denim jacket, black jeans, sneakers. I'm just Miranda the Mundane, come to see my friend. Wow, but I have a headache coming on, though. Too little sleep again. And I thought I was feeling a bit better when I woke up.

I go through the hallway, past a room where three boys are playing pool. One of them recognizes me from school and nods in a sort of half-polite, too-cool-for-you sort of way.

"I'm, ah, looking for Jade?" I say, hands in my pockets, trying to be nonchalant.

The boy nods again. "Out back," he says, pointing toward the yard.

"Thanks."

The trees are what give the Copper Beeches its name. There are at least ten of them, tall and purple-leafed, rising above the jungle of the garden. It's a sunny, breezy day and the wind is rustling the leaves. There's nobody else in sight. Frowning, I lean back against a tree that is gnarlier than the beeches. Not sure what it is, but it has low, spreading branches.

"Oi!"

I look around, startled. I can't see anyone behind me. Who spoke?

"Here, you idiot!"

I look up. Jade is sitting on a sort of wooden platform — a bit too rickety to be called a tree house — in the lower branches.

"How did you get up there?" I ask, and instantly realize what a stupid question that is.

"I flew, babe," says Jade sarcastically. "What do you think?" She narrows her eyes. "So, you found me, then."

"Um . . . yes. Sorry."

"Can't keep a secret round here, can we? Oh, unless you're Miss Miranda May, of course. *She's* full of them."

"Why didn't you tell me the truth about where you live?"

She gives a hollow laugh. "Oh, yeah. Like I'm gonna do that straightaway."

"I'm not judging you. How shallow do you think I am?"

"Sorry. It's just . . ." She clears her throat. "My parents . . . well, they split up. Me dad went back to Italy and nobody can find him. And Mum . . . she drinks."

"Drinks?" I say, confused. "Presumably she eats as well?"

Jade gives me the narrow-eyed treatment again. "Drinks alcohol, you idiot. As in, has a problem with it. As in, ain't fit to look after her own kid. Okay?" She sighs. "Come up, so we can talk."

I look for handholds on the trunk, and find one or two knobbly bits that I think I can hold on to. "Right. Hang on."

I haul myself up surprisingly easily and sit beside her.

"Sorry." I feel myself going red. "I'm —"

"A bit dim sometimes. I know."

"You told me your mum and dad worked from home. Running their own business, you said."

"Yeah, well, I lied, babe." Jade looks shifty. "My mum couldn't run a bath, let alone a business. I don't . . . like to tell too many people, y'know?"

"Okay. Yeah."

"I like it in this tree," says Jade. "I can spend hours up here and nobody ever finds me. Good, innit?"

I smile. "Everybody needs their own space." I pause. "So what's it like living here?"

She shrugs. "Not bad. Old Armitage is a bit of a dragon, but she's basically fair. What about you?"

"I'm okay." I smile weakly.

She prods me. "You eating all right? You look like you could do with some pies in you. You're not doing that stupid size-zero thing, are you?"

I wrinkle my nose. "Don't be daft. I just haven't been well."

She nods, looking away. I can't read her eyes.

We sit for a few minutes in silence. It feels comfortable not talking. It's almost like summer. We can hear gentle birdsong, and the faint sounds of the boys playing pool inside the house — the *click* of the balls, the occasional raised voice.

"Your dad died, didn't he?" she says softly.

I've not told her this yet. I was waiting for the right moment. I would ask her how she knows, but Jade's no fool. She keeps her ear to the ground, and it's not that hard to find out. As she said, you can't keep a secret around here.

"Yeah. He died last year."

"I used to quite like his show," she says.

"Thanks."

"I suppose you've got loads of them on DVD? So you can watch him over and over?"

"No . . . no, I wouldn't do that." It's funny how many people ask me this. "I mean, that was his work. He had a TV personality, you know? He put it on for work. Three-piece suit, and all the fake jokes. He wasn't like that at all. Not at home. He was . . . quiet, and kind, and gentle. And he loved my mum. Really loved her."

Now there's a silence that seems awkward.

"I've been in six schools before I came here," says Jade at last. She grins at me. "Kicked out of four, one closed, one burned down. And that weren't nothing to do with me," she adds hastily. "Nobody really seems to know what they wanna do with me, know what I mean?"

"Well, you're a handful."

"So they tell me."

"I expect they were glad to see the back of you," I say.

"Yeah, thanks for that." We smile at each other; she knows I'm only teasing. "It's . . . kind of hard to make friends," she says. "When you keep getting moved on."

"I can imagine."

"People don't easily trust me," she admits.

"Hey, I trust you."

"Do you?" She looks almost surprised.

"'Course I do."

But not enough to tell her what we're really doing, running after shadows, and not enough to tell her about my disturbing experience last night.

Jade jumps up and slithers down the trunk to the ground. "Come on. I want to show you something."

Inside, she takes me back through the games room and we wander into the back room where there are a couple of computers. Jade clicks the mouse, and a second later the Image-Ination software logo comes on the screen.

My eyes widen. "How did you get this?"

"Nicked it off school."

"Jade!" I look around, shocked, hoping nobody heard her.

"Chill out! It's not like anybody cares about some lame computer program, babe. Now . . . how about this?"

Jade clicks on to our school website, finds the smiling picture of the principal, Mr. Roseby, standing proudly in front of the school. She opens the Image-Ination window, imports the picture, and plays around with the settings for a minute or two.

"What shall we do?" she says. "I know."

She flips the picture back in. Instead of Mr. Roseby, there's now a picture of Jed Rock, lead singer of the JumpJets, standing in front of our school with his arms folded and a big grin on his face. All the shadows and the photo texture and everything are perfect — like he's really there.

I can't help laughing. "That is so cool!"

"Mr. Rock," she says. "Our new headmaster."

"If only. Can you imagine?"

Jade grins. "I reckon Miss Bellini would get on with him."

"Yeah." I look away, clear my throat, thinking that maybe I shouldn't talk about Miss Bellini in front of Jade. I might give stuff away.

She doesn't seem to notice. "Come on," she says. "Let's deface some more websites."

SEAVIEW HOTEL: WEDNESDAY 17:12

A cold wind batters the Esplanade as I skateboard along. The surface is good, not too many bumps or cracks, so I'm getting a smooth roll. Opposite the Seaview Hotel, I stop, kick the board up, and swing it from my fingers as I cross the road.

I can't help feeling I'm being watched.

Looking up and down the Esplanade, I can see a few people — families, kids, retirees — all doing their own thing, but not really paying me any attention. The sea is lashing the beach, cold and unfriendly, and there's a salty bite in the air today, along with the moldering smell of seaweed.

I take out the special pass Miss Bellini has given me — slim, matte black, the size of a bank card — and swipe it in the reader,

111

a little white box at about waist-height. The light on the white box goes from red to green, there's a *beep*, and the door clicks open.

I hurry inside, and the door closes behind me as I pick my way across the dusty, cobwebby hall, down the old stairs, into the underground parking lot and the Datacore. Everyone is there except Miss Bellini.

"You're late," says Cal, looking up from her computer as I clang down the metal staircase. She sounds tense.

I chuck my skateboard on the table. "Sorry. I had netball."

"It's Wednesday," says Cal, pausing with her plastic coffee cup halfway to her lips. "Netball is Tuesday."

I glower at her. "Extra netball. I need the practice."

Why do I lie? I don't know. Something about liking Jade, I guess, and feeling protective of my "normal" life with my friend. Not wanting them even to know about it, so they can't make fun of me for it.

"Can you please move *that*?" says Cal, pointing at my skateboard.

"A girl has to park her transport somewhere."

"Yes, well, not on the table, please. This isn't some tawdry little seaside café for Mundanes, you know."

"Sorr-*eee*," I say, sitting in the nearest chair and sticking my board underneath it.

Josh is standing by the illuminated map of Firecroft Bay, a notepad in his hand. He flashes me a grin. "Nice of you to join us."

"Okay," says Cal, swinging her hair. "Update, team?"

112

"I've isolated that Terminal Thirteen computer," says Ollie from his seat, "and cross-matched it with the user data." He holds up a strip of printouts and they fall to the floor like an enormous roll of toilet paper. "Want the short version, or the long version?"

Cal holds up her hand. "Brevity is a virtue."

"Sorry?"

"Short and sweet, Ollie. Minimum geek-speak."

Lyssa giggles. "She means she wants it in English!"

Ollie says, "That computer was being used by a readily identifiable log-in ID." He stabs at a button on the keyboard, and a face springs up on the monitor, picked out clearly in black and white.

I jump. I recognize the face immediately.

"So it was Jade's computer," I say, puzzled.

This is disturbing. I've just been talking to her, and now here we are, looking at her photo as if we're spying on her.

Josh waves a pencil at me. "Well done, Miranda. You have to get up early to get one past you."

Ignoring him, I peer at the screen. It looks like Jade's official school photo, date-stamped with the day she joined.

"Where did you get that?" I ask Ollie.

"Local authority records," he says. "We're all stamped, filed, and indexed these days, you know. In case any of us turns out to be, you know, a bit of a wacko."

I frown. "Nice thought. I take it the Civil Liberties people don't know about this?"

"They know nothing about *anything*," says Cal dismissively.

She sits down, gnawing the end of her pen. "So. We need to think about all this." She points at me suddenly. "Was Jade on the bus? That first morning?"

"Er . . ." I think hard, trying to remember. "Not sure."

Lyssa closes her eyes, as if trying to picture the scene. "No, I don't think she was."

"She wasn't," says Josh calmly. "I'd have remembered."

I can't help thinking there is something wrong about this conversation. It sounds rehearsed, like it's being put on for my benefit.

"She was definitely in the computer lab when the big zap happened," says Ollie.

For a moment there is silence.

"These energy surges," says Lyssa. "Interesting stuff."

"So . . . we keep an eye on her," says Josh. "Ollie's the surveillance expert. Why don't you go along with him, Miranda? Might learn a bit."

Ollie and I look at each other.

"I'm not very happy about it," I say uncertainly. "She's my friend."

It feels as if the world is tilting. Where do my loyalties truly lie? Nobody says anything. Four pairs of eyes are fixed on me.

I shrug, helplessly. I'm still the new girl, and it seems I have to do as I'm told. For now.

THE PIER: THURSDAY 15:43

"She hasn't moved for twenty-seven minutes."

I put down my teacup. "What?"

Ollie and I have been talking about this and that and the other for a bit, about computer games and TV and books, here in the Pier Café — and it's a surprise when he brings me back to business.

He flips his phone around to face me. "Jade Verdicchio," he says. "We're supposed to be watching her. Remember?"

"Oh, yeah. That." I look, uneasily, at the phone screen, which is showing a grainy image of Jade on a bench on the end of the pier, nibbling at a fluffy, pink stick of cotton candy. She is literally just around the corner from us — beyond the tacky shops and the bumper cars — but we're not watching her directly. "Ollie, how are you *doing* that?"

"Just tapping into the security camera feed," he says. "Easy when you've got a few hack codes."

"And you get those *how*, exactly?"

"Oh, you'd be surprised what a couple of upperclassmen geeks will swap for the rarest StarBreaker Gold Cards. The ones with the limited-edition watermark featuring their favorite babe, Angelica Dupree, playing Space Commander Nikki Tempest."

I smile. "Ah, and you think, because I'm not a geek, I'll be bamboozled by that. But I know enough about StarBreaker to know that the Gold Cards with the limited-edition watermark featuring Space Commander Nikki Thingy —"

"Tempest."

"Whatever . . . they were never actually *made*, were they? Or at least, only one ever was and it's in a sealed glass block in a safe in some famous comic store in New York. Am I right?"

Ollie grins. "They don't know that," he says.

I like talking to Ollie. He's the most normal of the Weirdos — sorry, my new friends. He isn't slinky and threatening like Cal, or a robot superbrain like Lyssa, or cool and superior like Josh. He's just a really smart, nerdy guy with a fantastic memory.

"So what are you *actually* giving these techno-geeks?"

"Well, they're Commander Nikki Tempest cards all right. Just . . . not exactly with a watermark. All right, all right. With a fake watermark." He leans back in his chair, as I pretend to be shocked. "C'mon, Miranda, it's so easy to fool these dudes. Seriously."

He glances at his phone. "Still not moved," he says with a sigh, and sips his Coke. "Where does your mum think you are tonight?"

"Philosophy Club."

"You are *kidding* me. She thinks King Eddie's has a *Philosophy Club?*"

"Seriously! My mum thinks I'm in the French Club, the Chess Club, the Astronomy Club . . . I'm running out of clubs!" I take a reassuring sip of tea. "I've got to go home and read something to make it look convincing."

"*Cogito ergo sum,*" Ollie intones.

"If you say so." I smile. "So, what brought you into this, Ollie?"

He smiles, not looking as if he doesn't want to answer, exactly, but not quite meeting my gaze. "Aaaah, y'know . . . this and that."

I shake my head. "What and what?"

He shrugs. "I moved here three years ago," he says. "Me and my mum and dad. Perfectly normal family. Except for the fact that my big sister had disappeared."

I'm stunned. "Ollie, I'm so sorry. Are the police following it up?"

"Oh, the police did what they could. But when I say Bex disappeared, I mean *literally* disappeared. I don't mean she went missing on the way home from school or on a camping trip or anything like that. I mean she popped out of existence."

There's a new look on his face, one I haven't seen before. He's keeping it under control, but I can see the sadness there.

"How?"

"It was Bonfire Night. I was, what, nine. She was eleven. I was standing on one side of the village bonfire, burning hot, seeing how close I could get with a marshmallow on a stick."

"As is the Bonfire Night tradition," I encourage him.

"Yeah. And I looked up, and I could see Bex, just around the corner of the fire from me, partly hidden by the smoke. And then . . ." Ollie shakes his head. "I've gone through this a thousand times in my head, and it still doesn't seem quite real."

"Go on," I say gently.

"Miranda, I swear I saw Bex *vanish*. One second she was standing there, the next she was gone. Like someone had flicked a switch and turned her off. Pop."

We're the only customers in the café. It's silent apart from the boy serving behind the counter, drumming his fingers on the till.

117

"Of course, I tried to tell my mum and dad, and the police," Ollie says, "but it's not the kind of story you can easily get people to believe. Nine-year-old boy, plays a lot of video games, reads a lot of books, overactive imagination . . . You can see what they thought. Typical grown-ups. So literal." He looks me in the eye. "She wasn't *abducted*, Miranda. Not like they said. On a November evening, in the middle of a crowded field, the whole village there? Kids on bikes all over the place, teenagers hanging round at the gates? *Someone* would have seen. No way could anyone have taken an eleven-year-old kid out of that place."

I nod. "We all know the Stranger Danger drill."

"Yes, and I know Bex. She'd have been spitting, swearing, kicking. She'd have been screaming, *'That's not my dad,'* the way you're told." He finishes his Coke. "Nah. Something happened that night. Something that ordinary science can't explain."

"I'm so sorry."

"And then we came here. New start. All that. But I got a sense there was something special about this place the moment we arrived. And then I started at the school, and everything was just normal, until Miss Bellini started last term. One lunchtime, when I was helping her fix a disk error, it all came out. Bex, the bonfire, all of it. And you know what, Miranda? *She believed me.*" Ollie leans back, shaking his head, blowing his cheeks out. "It makes me . . . when I think about it . . . I just wanted to . . . you know? She was the first adult ever to believe me. To listen and to actually think I wasn't making it up."

"Could she do anything?"

"Not directly. But she said she knew of things like that happening. So that's when it all started to snowball. And I met Cal and Josh. And Lyssa came along later. The stuff we do, Miranda, the things we investigate, I'm kind of hoping that, somewhere buried inside it all, there's an answer about Bex."

"I hope so, too," I say softly.

"And you?" he says. "Who did you lose?"

Startled, I feel my heart skip a beat. I'm about to say something, when he glances at his phone and his face turns to shock. He leaps to his feet and grabs his coat. "Come on!"

I don't have time to see what he has seen, but I rush out of the café, following him along the pier, our feet thudding on the wood, until we are there at the very end, as far out as you can go in Firecroft Bay without hitting the water. Jade's climbed up onto the lowest rung of the barrier. We skid to a halt, and she turns around and sees us.

Ollie whispers, "She looked like she was about to —"

"What?" snaps Jade, jumping down. "Chuck myself over the edge? Is that what you thought? Hello, Miranda. Nice of you to let me know you were coming to the pier. I might have come with you."

I look down, blushing. "It's . . . I mean . . . It's not . . ."

"No, I bet." Her voice is cold and steely. "Hello, Weirdo Boy," she says to Ollie.

"It's Ollie."

119

"Sure. Mind if I still just call you Weirdo Boy? It helps my concentration. What you got, then, Weirdos? Spit it out. What you got?"

"Got?" I ask.

"Yeah. I mean, it's obviously Let's Investigate Gypsy Girl Day, so what've you found out?" She comes right up to us, arms folded, chewing ostentatiously, her earrings glinting in the sun. "Yeah, my gran was a Romany, a Gypsy. Yeah, my dad's an unemployed lay-about who can't be bothered to leave his new girlfriend in Italy an' come an' see his own daughter. And yeah, my mum's best mate's named Gordon's Gin, and some days she can barely remember her own name. And nobody wants to foster me because I'm too 'difficult,' apparently. You got enough now?"

"Come on, let's go," I say to Ollie.

She glares at me. "What do you *want*? So much for being friends."

"She's perfectly normal," Ollie says, disappointed, monitoring readouts on his phone. "A boring Mundane. There's not even a trace of any unusual activity around her. And yet she *was* the one using PC Terminal Thirteen."

I look her in the eye.

"I'm really sorry, Jade," I say. "Please, Ollie, let's leave her alone."

Jade tosses her empty cotton candy stick into the sea and glares at us. "Do they let you lot out for the day?" she snarls. "I mean, seriously, are you all mental or what . . . ? 'Boring Mundane' . . . I mean, for real?"

"We're wasting time, here, Miranda," Ollie says. He nods at Jade. "Sorry to have got in your way," he says. "We won't bother you again."

"No," says Jade coldly. "You won't." And she stalks off toward the amusement arcades without even looking at me.

I notice Ollie has taken control here. It isn't till he is ready to leave that we do.

We set off back down the pier, through the noise and the crowds and the sugary smells. We pass a tattooed couple having a furious row. A woman drags a screaming toddler along, the kid's ice cream dripping onto the wooden boards.

I am quiet, hating myself.

"Well, it's not her," Ollie says. "Maybe, whoever's doing all this, they're managing to mask themselves somehow. Hide it from us. But no, not her, not Terminal Thirteen. Too obvious." He stops, shrugs. "Sorry to have wasted your afternoon. And sorry about . . ." He nods back along the pier. ". . . you know."

Despite it all, I manage to smile. "It wasn't a waste. It was pretty informative for me, Ollie."

"I think we all need to meet up on Saturday," he says. "Miss Bellini's talking about some book she wants to show us. She's got to get it from London, apparently. The British Library."

We've reached the beach end of the pier now. I push my hair out of my eyes. "You can't just take stuff out of the British Library. Can you?"

Ollie grins. "Miss Bellini can do anything." He gives me a

salute. "See you later," he says. "And thanks for the chat. It was . . . well, you know."

I nod and wave back as he heads off. I watch him disappear down the seafront, waiting until his bright blond hair has vanished into the crowd, and then I head home.

CHAPTER TEN

stone

THE OLD VICARAGE: THURSDAY 23:39

I've looked up the word *nightmare*.

It's nothing to do with a mare, not the horsey kind. It's from the Old English *maere*, meaning an evil goblin or spirit, and it's linked to a verb that means "to destroy, bruise, or crush." In some versions I've read, the spirit is specifically female. The *maere* would sit on your chest and make you feel as if you were being suffocated. Not cool.

Then the other day I found this picture in an art book in the library, by a bloke called Fuseli. It shows a woman in white, sort of damsel-in-distress type, spread out on her bed in some long nightdress. Her head's hanging down over the edge. Looks pretty uncomfortable. And the squat little goblin-troll-thing is sitting on her stomach with this horrible expression on its face. It gave me the creeps.

I had to slam the book shut. Everybody in the library looked up, and Miss Challis peered at me over her glasses.

But I'm awake now, when my phone rings.

Luckily, I have it on silent, but I can see it flashing, the vibrations almost moving it off my bedside table. I check the caller ID. It's Josh. Why's he calling me this late? Doesn't make sense.

"*What?*"

"Well, that doesn't sound very nice, Miranda," he says. "Aren't you pleased to hear from me?"

"Josh, it's nearly midnight. Most normal people are in bed. What do you *want?*"

"What I want is for you to put some warm clothes on and hop out of your window."

"Sorry?"

I am pretending to be annoyed with him, but my heart is racing in anticipation. Things like this never used to happen to me. Bedtime was bedtime. The thrill of a midnight adventure is too great to resist.

"Well, it should be pretty easy. That porch roof under your window has a pretty gentle incline to the driveway."

I scramble to the curtains and peek through the gap. I can see him out there beyond the gates, under the streetlight. He does a mock salute.

"What are you doing outside my house?"

"Bring a flashlight."

"I'm not coming."

But I don't even convince myself, let alone him, and anyway I'm smiling as I say it.

Two minutes later, I'm scrambling down the roof in black jeans, boots, sweater, and a knit cap, feeling like a cat burglar.

I teeter on the edge by the gutter for a second or two. The night air is bitingly cold. Clouds pass across the moon, so the light seems to move in the yard like a living thing. I jump.

I remember to flex my legs, and the landing is surprisingly painless. I'm more worried about the crunching noise my Doc Martens make on the gravel as I land.

I glance up at Mum's study window. There's a soft orange light on. She's still up, working.

I just have to hope she doesn't decide go in and check on me.

THE ABBEY: FRIDAY 00:01

"Just gone midnight," I say, glancing down at Josh. He's crouching by the great oak doors of the Abbey, doing something with a screwdriver. "It's officially Friday."

"Need your beauty sleep, Miranda?" he says. "You can always go home. You look a bit tired."

"Yeah, so everyone keeps saying. I'm fine. Look, why didn't we get the others out? Cal could have that door open in a second with that phone . . . doodah-thing."

"No, she couldn't. Ollie hacked the school security system, and this lock is Victorian. It's simple but effective." He looks up. "And I was asked to come and take a look here on my own. But I thought I'd bring you along."

"Why? What's this about?"

"Tell you in a minute," he says, concentrating on the door.

"Well, hurry up! It's cold! And if a police car comes along . . ."

I've pulled my black knit cap down as low as I dare, trying to hide my face.

Josh grins. "You worry too much, Miranda. There isn't a curfew in this town, you know."

"I should be in bed, dreaming sweet dreams." I wince. "Ollie and I followed Jade down to the pier after school, did he say? He worked out she's nothing to do with all this."

"Yeah, I know. Quiet, I'm working."

I make a face at him. The lock makes a *click*. He pushes the Abbey door, and it opens with a slight creak.

"The doors of the Lord are open to all," he says with quiet satisfaction, spreading his hands. "Even if you sometimes need to break and enter."

"This is against the *law*, you know."

"Oh, give it a rest." He does a yakking mouth sign with his hand, but thankfully doesn't see the gesture I give him in return. "You've got one mouth and two ears for a reason, Miranda."

"Yeah, well, my mouth isn't as big as yours. And it doesn't usually talk rubbish."

Inside, we shut the wooden door behind us. The Abbey is not welcoming. It's vast, cavernous, and chilly. There's something about it that makes me feel a curling, twisting coldness inside, like I've swallowed an ice cube.

A few candles flicker in alcoves, not giving out much light but throwing wobbly shadows across the nave. There's a smell of polished wood and centuries of use.

"Go on, then," I say. "Why are we here?"

"Signals," he says. "Odd . . . fluctuations in the Convergence. Ollie and Lyssa have been getting some energy blips triangulated on the Abbey. I've been saying for a couple of days that I'd check them out."

"What kind of *blips*?"

"Pyroelectric ones. Electricity discharged as a result of rapid rises and drops in temperature."

I feel myself turning even colder as he says it. There's definitely some stuff linking up, clicking together in my mind here. Heat and cold. Electricity and exchange of energy. I ought to listen better in Science.

He wanders up the nave and shines his flashlight about randomly. "You know," he says, "a few years back some scientists in America did this really cool thing. An experiment. They played twelve subjects a YouTube clip of a basketball game, asking them to watch carefully and count the number of passes made by each team."

"Is this actually going to be interesting and relevant?" I ask, hurrying after him.

"Yes. Shut up. Now, the interesting thing was this: At one point during the action, a man in a gorilla costume comes onto the basketball court."

"A man in a *what*?"

"*Gorilla* costume," repeats Josh firmly.

We walk on up the nave, picking out the darkest corners with our flashlights.

"He moved quite slowly among the players, right? Staying in full view of the camera for at least thirty seconds. *None* of the viewers commented on the gorilla at all." He takes a deep breath. "When the researchers played the clip back to them in slow motion and showed them what they had missed seeing, they couldn't believe it. Lots of them even refused to believe that it was the same clip."

"And it was?"

"It was."

"Why a gorilla costume?" I ask, whispering.

"It doesn't have to be a gorilla costume!" he hisses. "The point is that it was something weird, incongruous. And nobody noticed, because *they were looking for the wrong thing*. It's called *inattentional blindness*. That's Mundanes for you. They just don't notice stuff. But we notice, because we know."

He holds up a hand, and we stop.

"What?"

"Thought I heard something." He shrugs. "Maybe not."

"So what are we looking for?"

"This place has been here nearly six hundred years, Miranda, and it's hardly changed. Firecroft Bay was a little harbor village when it was built. Which makes it the perfect place."

"For what?"

"Echoes," says Josh. "Of the past, the present. Places like this are key points on the Convergence." He looks up toward an ornate screen between two small side altars and points at a small lantern hanging there. It appears to have a candle inside burning with a blue flame. "Now, what's that doing there?"

I frown. "I don't know. You don't normally see anything like that in a church. How is it blue?"

"Some sort of copper compound, I expect."

"Oh, chemistry. Good old Miss Bellini," I say with a grin.

He stands beneath the lantern. "A ghost light," he says softly.

"Ghost light?"

"Yeah. They put them in theaters when all the other lights are off. People thought they'd ward off the evil spirits. Of course, some say they were just to stop the last person out from tripping up and going head-first into the orchestra pit."

"That sounds more likely," I say.

He frowns. "Never seen one on hallowed ground before, though. That's really odd."

"You're showing off your knowledge now."

"Not really." He walks around the ghost light, ducks under it, peers up at it. "It's good in patches. I've often been told I've got a photographic memory. But it's not like Lyssa's. Mine's, well, amateur photographic. Lots of blurred birthday parties, all out of focus, people with heads and feet cropped off. Six months totally missing from when I was eight, because I kept the lens cap on."

"Very funny."

While Josh is examining the ghost light, I walk over to a small array of flickering candles. I light one, putting a coin into the box.

"Special time of year?" he asks, surprisingly softly.

"My dad. It's . . . coming up to the first anniversary." I sit down in the nearest pew.

"Ah."

"I used to go to church when I was a little girl, when I didn't know I had a choice. I'd swing my legs, and fidget, and just think about the roast potatoes and the chicken and the thick brown gravy that were always waiting when we got home. Dad cooked it. He didn't come to church. He said he liked God to be personal."

Josh is listening.

"Just after it happened, Reverend Watson, our vicar, told me not to be angry at God, you know? I'd never have thought of that, if she'd not said it."

I pull my jacket closely around me, aware that I'm shivering a little. The Abbey seems to have become colder, and the shadows between the pillars and pews are growing darker and longer. I feel lost and lonely in this great, dark stone building. It seems like an awfully long time since I was a little girl.

Josh comes over and squats beside me, at the edge of the pew. For a moment there is silence. We hear what might be a pigeon fluttering high up in the roof. Then he asks something that would seem odd from anyone else.

"Do you ever *see* him?"

I think long and hard before I answer.

"Okay," I say carefully. "I'm, like, crazy telling you, but . . . there was once, just before Christmas, in London. I was looking in the shop windows on Oxford Street. It was just getting dark. I thought I saw . . . a reflection."

Josh nods. There is no trace of disbelief or mockery in his eyes. "Go on," he says.

"Well, there was a gap in the crowd for a second. I was sure I'd seen . . ." I shake my head. "It wasn't him." I frown, look up suddenly. "Is it me, or is it getting . . . ?"

The Abbey seems to have grown not only colder but also dimmer. I gaze up at the carved pulpit, the painted Virgin Mary, wondering why it all makes me feel so uneasy.

Josh goes back to the ghost light, and stares down the nave.

"*Miranda!*"

Shocked by his sharp tone of voice, I leap up and hurry over to him.

"Have you noticed anything odd?" he says softly.

"Apart from the cold? Not really. It's an old building. Wind must get in all the time. Through the cracks."

I am lying, though. It's more than just the cold. There's a tingling inside me. It feels somehow . . . unearthly.

Josh points toward the huge oak doors at the front of the church. "There were two candles alight by that door when we came in," he says.

I realize what he is saying. The whole of that end of the nave is now in darkness. And as we watch, candles start flickering.

Then, one by one, they start going out.

I grab Josh's sleeve. "Are you doing that? Tell me you're doing that."

"I'm not doing that."

It's as if invisible fingers are pinching the wicks.

Pop. Pop. Pop.

The last to go is the ghost light. Darkness spreads like a stain across the Abbey.

We both switch our flashlights on to full beam, without saying a thing.

"You all right, Miranda?"

"Yes," I manage.

The arches in the highest reaches of the Abbey begin to darken. There is a sound of wind — no, not wind, more like a low murmur, a rustling, as if many voices are whispering urgently to one another.

And then, in the echoing space, the singing begins.

CHAPTER ELEVEN

enemies

THE ABBEY: FRIDAY 00:21

Ring around the rosie.

It's a young girl's voice — tremulous but clear. I am absolutely shaking in terror, because I know the song and I know the voice, even though I've never heard anything like it. The sound is old and new, young and ancient, clear and yet somehow cracked like old stone.

The most terrifying thing of all is that the voice is reaching into me. It's singing as if it knows me. The rhyme echoes up through the Abbey, filling the space, bouncing off the walls.

I look at Josh. He has heard it, too.

But he isn't scared. He looks totally fascinated, and he's holding up his phone — recording it all, I guess. I'm glad he's got the presence of mind, because I haven't.

"Time to get out of here?" suggests Josh, looking intently at me.

The voice is distorting now, sounding squashed and metallic as if it's been auto-tuned.

I try to move my legs, to break into a run, but for some reason my body won't obey my brain. My feet are glued to the floor.

133

"Come on, come on!" Josh says.

I look at him in despair and realize he's equally rooted to the spot.

"Block it out!" he snaps, and puts his hands over his ears.

I do the same, muffling the sounds of the singing. Finally, my right foot peels itself from the floor and I drag it along, a lead weight. It's like one of those dreams where you're running and can't get away.

Concentrate.

Life comes back to my right leg, and then my left.

I glance at Josh. He nods. We grab each other's hands and run full tilt for the oak doors.

The singing voice seems to chase after us, gathering momentum like a vast tidal wave of sound.

We skid to a halt.

The way to the door is blocked. *Something has appeared.*

At first it's only half visible, half formed. A shimmering column of grayish light, flickering in the darkness, like a ghostly candle. And then, with a rush of cold air and an evil smell like rotting flesh, the shimmering blur turns into something more solid. A wizened, yellow face, twisted like bark and covered in pustules. A hunched body swathed in dark robes and long, dark hair.

The Shape. But more than that now.

The first thing I think of saying is, "Can you see it, too?"

"Oh, yes," he says softly, almost absently. He doesn't know how important that is to me. Someone else seeing my Shape now.

The Shape seems to hiss and wave an arm.

I jump backward, but Josh is taking shot after shot on his phone. "Any ideas?" he mutters.

And that's when I get this stupid thought.

"Okay. Just one," I say.

"Knock yourself out."

I reach for the nearest pew and pull out a leather-bound Bible, embossed in gold with a cross.

"You've got to be kidding," says Josh. "You've seen too many bad vampire films."

"It's not the cross," I say. "It's what it stands for. Belief sets up a protective barrier."

"I don't think that's going to work. Do you believe in it?"

"Well, I'm kind of unresolved. Let's find out."

I need to confront this thing. I need to do something. I've told the others most of what I know, but I'm still the one who senses the terror, the one who sees it in dreams.

I hold the book up like a shield and swing it from side to side.

The Shape pulses, but doesn't vanish.

"Throw it," says Josh.

"What?"

"Throw it!"

And he grabs the Bible from me and hurls it into the swirling gray light.

The book crackles with energy as it bounces off its — her? — body, and stays, twisting in the air, for a second. Then, in the grip of some icy wind, it begins to peel away, layer by layer. First the leather cover is ripped from its binding, curls up and falls like a withered leaf to the floor. As one page after another peels off, the Bible turns banana yellow and crumbles to dust. There is a pungent odor of burning leather and a damp smell of decaying paper. The Shape seems, for a moment, to fold in on itself, as if bending over in some kind of pain.

Josh and I both stare in astonishment for a second, then we take our chance and run for the main doors.

Josh throws himself against them, pushing them open, and once we are both out in the night air again, he slams them shut.

The sounds from inside the Abbey are suddenly cut off, as if someone has thrown a switch.

And we keep running.

We don't stop until we are down by the Esplanade, leaning over the barrier, gasping for breath. Beyond, the sea roars.

Behind us, there are the sounds of dying nightlife — a few revving motorbikes, some people being turned out of bars, a radio blaring somewhere. Two lads, drunk and laughing, swagger past us and don't give us a second look.

I have the whole of the English language, or at least what I know of it, to express what we've just seen. The language of Shakespeare and a million other writers.

But all I can manage to do on this occasion is gasp.

He claps me on the shoulder. "You said it, Miranda. You said it." Laughing, he holds his phone up to scan through the images.

"What did it do?" I gasp, still getting my breath back. "To the Bible?"

He shrugs. "Some kind of molecular discharge, I imagine. Interfacing with the physical world and releasing concentrated entropy."

"Oh. Great. How about translating that into English for me?" I notice he is staring at his phone screen, not listening to me. "What's up?" I ask.

Josh shows me. The screen is blank.

"Nothing," he says. "The entire memory — it's been wiped."

KING EDWARD VI HIGH SCHOOL: FRIDAY 12:10

The school is humming with the usual lunchtime commotion: thundering feet, shouting and catcalling, the crashing of crockery and scraping of chairs and tables. It all echoes in my head.

I am exhausted from last night, and feeling like I'm definitely coming down with something, but I am trying to rise above it, trying to pretend it doesn't exist.

Jade is being okay with me. It's almost like the pier incident never happened.

I don't understand or deserve it. I should be grateful but right now I can't really give my mind to her problems.

"So, the thing is," says Jade, prattling away to me as we clatter down the stairs, "Ryan Crofts is kind of saying he wants to go out with me. Now, do I go out with him because he says he wants to go out with me, or is that, like, too sad? I mean, it looks a bit needy,

137

don't it . . . ? I mean, Ryan Crofts is all right, but he's a bit, well, full of himself." She stops dead so several other pupils almost cannon into her. Someone mutters "pikey" at her as they push past her, but for once she ignores them. "Babe, are you listening to me at all?"

"No. Sorry. Not really."

I can't kid myself. I've not been able to concentrate all day. I know my work is worthless. Maybe I'm getting the flu.

Jade is peering at me. "Either pale foundation is really in with the Weirdos this week, or you need to lie down, babe."

"Um . . . yeah." I slump against the lockers, feeling dizzy.

I feel Jade's arm catch me before I slide.

"Come on," she says. "You need to go to the nurse's."

I do go to the nurse's, and what's more I go home. Miss Bellini orders me to. And once I'm there, I crawl straight into bed. By now, the time on my watch says 12:54.

This thing — this gift, this power, whatever it is — seems to be draining the strength out of me. It's like I am newly connected to something and still stabilizing all my settings.

THE OLD VICARAGE: FRIDAY 16:17

I wake up feeling better. Mum, still convinced that I've just got a cold, has brought me some hot lemon tea.

I go out onto the landing. Mum's just put Truffle down for his afternoon nap and I can hear him snoozing and snuffling happily in his room. I go in and look. Little hands above his head, little pink face soft and warm and contented. He can be an annoying whiner when he's awake, but in his crib he is always a little angel. I lean down and kiss him. "Sweet dreams, Truffle," I murmur, then tiptoe out of his room.

The doorbell makes me jump. I duck back into the shadow of Truffle's room and listen as Mum goes down the hall. I hear the door open.

"Hello, Mrs. May," says a familiar voice. "I'm Callista, from school. I've just come to drop off a book for Miranda. I hope she's feeling a little better?"

"Come on in," says Mum. "I think she could do with some company." She calls upstairs. "Miranda! Friend of yours!"

I'm shocked. Why is Cal here? Something must be happening.

I hear Mum taking Cal into the dining room. "You girls will have to excuse me — I've got some work to do. There's tea in the pot."

I come downstairs and find Cal at the dining-room table. She's been home to change after school — she's wearing a loose white top and her hair's in a bun with wisps artfully hanging down.

"Hi," I say.

"Hello." She smiles, but it feels artificial.

I pour cups of tea for both of us.

"Your hands are shaking," says Cal. She looks at me with her sharp green eyes. "Are you sure you're quite well, Miranda?"

"Yes . . . yes, fine. What did you want to talk to me about?"

"Nothing, really," she says. "I just wanted to see you. You know, outside the rough-and-tumble of school. Josh says you had quite an encounter at the Abbey." She keeps her gaze fixed on me as I reply.

"Yeah, I've emailed Miss B. It's in the report. With all the encryptions you showed me."

Doing written reports on our activities should seem like extra homework, but it doesn't. It's thrilling, exciting. It makes me feel important, and wanted.

Cal nods. "We're getting somewhere. Good teamwork." She leans across the table, suddenly, and holds my arm too firmly for comfort. I stare down at her hand. "Miranda. Listen. If any of this makes you feel . . . upset, or worried . . . you'll talk to us, won't you? To me, or Miss B, or Josh? Because so few people get this chance. Don't mess it up."

I'm surprised by this passionate outburst, but I don't let it show. "Of course," I tell her calmly. "I won't mess up."

"Don't hold anything back from us," she says. She looks straight at me as if she's trying to bore right into my mind. There's something older about her again, something scary and unsettling.

"Of . . . of course. Look, everything's recorded, like I said."

"I don't want to upset you, Miranda."

"You're not." I look down pointedly. "But you are hurting my arm a bit."

Cal slowly releases her grip but she goes on staring at me. "What we deal with, it's not the kind of thing you'll ever have encountered before. But that test in the Seaview showed you were the right one for us."

My mum comes bustling in, searching for something in the folders on the bookshelf. "Don't mind me, girls," she says absently.

"Mrs. May," says Cal with icy politeness. "So kind of you to make tea."

Mum glances over her shoulder and smiles. "Sarah, please," she says. "Everyone calls me Sarah."

"How long have you been in your line of work, Sarah?" Cal asks.

"Since just after Miranda was born," Mum answers, pulling down a folder and putting her glasses on to scribble some notes. "I was in industry before. But holistic therapy — it suddenly seemed the right thing to do."

"People need answers, right?" says Cal. "Outside what they call the conventional methods. A good place for it, this."

Mum looks up briefly from her folder. "The ancient beliefs are still strong, you know. There's a lot about them that still holds true."

"This town is full of that stuff, though, isn't it?" Cal says. "The ley lines converging, and the old barrows up on the hills, and the legends about the fishermen's ghosts in the harbor . . . legends of witchcraft and the Plague."

I look uneasily from my mother to Cal and back again. It's almost as if they are playing a game with this conversation, each trying to make the other reveal something.

"Well, that's Britain for you," says Mum with a smile, not looking Cal in the eye. "A great country steeped in folklore."

Cal's not going to let it go. "But there's almost more of that than of your thing. You know. More old shadows and mystery than healing and balance. Do you think that's your job? Kick out the old, ring in the new?"

What is she *doing*? It's almost like Cal is trying to goad my mum into a response. Trying to get her to say something she can savage.

Mum seems more amused, though, than anything. One hand on her hip, she asks, "What are you trying to say, Callista?"

Cal holds up her hands defensively. "Nothing. Just, you know . . . of all the harbor towns you could have come and worked in . . . what a coincidence you end up here." She shrugs, puts her bottom lip out, and blows a puff of air. "Y'know."

Mum looks very serious, peering over her half-frame glasses at Cal, and for a moment I feel a strange chill.

"I knew the history of this place," she says quietly. "We all know the stories of the old beliefs. You can't come and do my work in somewhere so full of ancient legends and curses and not be aware of it all." She snaps the folder shut. "It just makes my work all the more interesting."

"Really?" says Cal casually. She catches my eye, and I blush.

"I'd love to carry on the debate, Callista," Mum says with a smile, "but I really do have lots of work to get through." With a swish of skirt and a jangle of bangles, she's gone.

Once she's out in the hall, I lean across the table, curious to find out what Cal was up to. "You've got to be careful!" I snap. "I can't have her finding out!"

"About our shadow chasing?" Cal asks, lifting her teacup. "Or about you seeing things?"

I fold my arms and scowl. "Both."

Cal is like a sleek, powerful wildcat — one you want on your side, not cornering you in a forest clearing with its fangs bared and its claws unsheathed. She has a dangerous edge.

She grins. "Don't worry. We've all got secrets to keep."

"Really?"

"Yeah. Take Josh, for example. There's a story there. About him having to leave St. Xavier's and come to our school. His dad's working abroad. In financial trouble, someone told me. Lost his money in one of those banking crises." Cal leans back, shaking her head. "But I think there's more to it. And his mum . . . well, she's just a bit odd."

"And what about you?" I ask. I remember what Josh told me on the beach, about her mum and stepdad not having time for her.

"Me?" Cal gives me an innocent smile. "I'm fine."

"You were the first person to talk to me at the bus stop. I don't reckon that was a coincidence. Whatever there is in me . . . you sensed it, didn't you?"

Cal leans back, looking for a moment as if she is not going to answer. "Perhaps," she says. "Perhaps not. I'm usually good with objects, rather than people. I can often . . . read them. Where they've been, who they've been with, and so on. History." She shrugs. "It just comes naturally."

The computer, and the bus. She mentioned the psychic imprint of an owner on an object, I remember.

"My mum and stepdad have never known," she goes on. "They

wouldn't really be interested, anyway. Running the pub means they work seven days a week. I think they're just glad I've got hobbies to keep me busy."

"Is that what all this is? A hobby?"

"Before Miss Bellini found me, I felt like a freak," she says. "This doesn't help, does it? Kids say nasty things. If you're fat, or pimply, or wear glasses or braces . . . Anyway, I . . . had a bit of trouble. I went a bit . . . weird. Dad left home. I spent some time with some doctors."

"Sorry to hear that."

I know the kind of doctors she must mean. Not the sort who mend broken arms and dish out rash cream, but the ones who look after your head. Who take care of your mind.

"Nah, it's all fine now. I've got a purpose in life. Just like the others, you see."

"And then there's me."

"Yeah," she says softly. "It's like we've been waiting for you. All this time."

There's something a bit odd about the way she says that to me, almost menacing. It puts me on my guard. I wouldn't confide in her, the way I would in Josh.

"Anyway." She quickly finishes her tea. "Thank your mother for me. Don't forget the team meeting tomorrow morning. And don't be late. Miss B's got something good to show us."

"I'm supposed to be —"

Cal interrupts me, her voice hard. "You're supposed to be with us. Make something up."

There's a moment's tense silence as we look at each other across the table.

"See you tomorrow, then," I mutter.

Cal hoists her bag on her shoulder. "I'll see myself out," she says, and turns away from me with a casual toss of her head.

In the living room, I slump on the sofa, flicking through TV channels, seeing the images but taking nothing in.

It's odd. I get the feeling that conversation with Cal was always on the verge of being about something else.

Something far more important.

Something she wanted to say, but couldn't.

CHAPTER TWELVE

animus

MILLENNIUM ESTATE: SATURDAY 09:42

Even after I was off school for the afternoon, they assume I'm going to be straight back in the swing of things. Before the meeting with Miss Bellini, I get a text telling me to meet Josh by the war memorial on the Millennium Estate.

Groaning, I haul myself out of bed, splashing my face. I just about feel human. In the bathroom mirror, I look pale, but not terrible. Downstairs, I grab my jacket, shout to Mum that I'm going out to meet friends, and don't even hear what she says as I hurry down the steps and head for the Millennium Estate at a brisk pace. I check my watch, guessing it will take about ten minutes. I'm right.

He barely looks at me as I arrive, but strides off down the middle of the street. "It's on the run," he says. "That thing. It knows we're onto it, and yet it never strays far. I wonder *why?*"

My heartbeat quickens at the way he says it. So, we're hunting it now. Tracking it down. This is a change of approach.

I feel like a cowboy in a Western, walking into town for a showdown. Josh's long, dark coat flutters in the breeze. He's got something different with him this time — a piece of Miss Bellini's gear. It's like a flashlight, but with a wider end shaped like a big bagel, and with a small digital screen built into it.

We're not far from Craghollow Park and the school. Just a few streets away, in fact, from the Copper Beeches Children's Home where Jade lives. The houses all look the same — smart little semis with neat gardens and short drives. I'm reminded of a song Dad used to play to me on the CD player: "Little boxes, on the hillside . . ."

Panting, we stop, and I rest my hands on my knees and look up at Josh.

"This is the point where you say something daft like, 'I think we should split up,' right?"

He grins. "You and I watch the same films. Listen, if you want to hunt, even chasing shadows, you have to hunt *efficiently*. Same reason we never get the police involved. Dogs, guns, radios . . . all those things cause more problems than they solve."

I take a few deep breaths. "So what is that?" I ask, nodding at the device.

"It's an ultrasonic motion resonator," he says.

"You just made that up."

"Well, I didn't want to call it a magic spook-detector."

"So what is it?"

Josh grins at me. "A magic spook-detector," he says.

"You're kidding me. Again."

"No, no. I swear on my mother's grave."

"Your mother's not dead," I point out. "As far as I know."

"She's got a grave, though." Josh winces and shakes his head. "Well, a headstone. She's had it made and left the year of death blank. Trust me, it's a long story. I'll tell you one day."

I stare at him. It's hard to know sometimes when he is being serious.

"This," he says, tapping the ultra-whatsit rezza-thingy, "records all unusual signals in the paranormal range. Including pyro-electric energy, like we detected at the Abbey."

It's a bright and sunny day, and everything seems picked out in unnatural, cartoon colors. We can hear birds singing. There's pink and white blossoms in the trees, some of it carpeting the ground like confetti. At the end of the road, there's an old man washing his car with a soapy sponge. I can hear someone bouncing a soccer ball against a garage door. It's suburban peace.

"Too quiet," Josh says.

"Then why is *that* thing flashing?" I ask.

"Huh?" Josh holds up the resonator and turns slightly, trying to see where the signal gets weaker and stronger.

I blink.

And then I have one of those moments.

Just like when I was going to be hit by the truck. When I knew it was coming even though I hadn't seen it or heard it. And just like when I was in the Pod with Miss Bellini, and I was able to say just by thinking, just by imagining, which of the hemispheres the white ball was under. And like in the Abbey. At the edge of my perception. A sense that hasn't been invented or given a name yet.

It's a flash of *darkness*, like a smudge on reality, but also a coldness and a screech inside my head. My eyes aren't open or closed, but I feel as if I am awake-dreaming, there in the middle of the road. I'm breathless and hot.

I am standing on the edge of a field, and behind me is a blazing forest, a huge dark finger of black smoke pointing up into the sky. A girl with dark hair is running in slow motion across a scarred, burned field. Running, running. I can hear horses, but cannot see them. There is soot and smoke around her, but she doesn't appear to be burned herself.

I gasp, and my eyes are back in Firecroft Bay.

I blink. For a second, I still feel unbearably hot, and my eyes are stinging as if from bonfire smoke.

Then I'm staring down the road toward the park.

There are pockets of shadow gathering around the play equipment. Dark, deep shadows like you expect to get at midday in the middle of summer.

"Josh," I say cautiously.

He's still turning in a 360-degree circle, surveying the estate. "Again . . . not straying far . . ."

"*Jossssh!*" I hiss.

He's angling the resonator toward Craghollow Park. The trace is fluctuating, but there is a wavering blue light when he points it in a direct line down the middle of the road, through the gate and toward —

The swings.

Beside me, Josh is still blathering on. "I was checking archive records earlier. This whole area has strong links to the past. First of all, I looked up the Abbey."

"Uh-huh. Big gray stone place. You can't miss it." My eyes are still fixed on the shadows by the swings.

"Very funny. You know that land was a burial ground for victims of the Black Death? Before they built the Abbey over the site, the bishop came to sprinkle the whole place with holy water first. And then here — the Crag Hollows, it was called — was a place where they used to burn witches in the time of the Plague. The area was untouched for centuries, until the park and the estate were built on top of it in the nineteen fifties."

I glance at the resonator readout, then stare hard into the shadows of the park.

There is someone standing beside the swings.

No, there isn't —

I narrow my eyes. Yes, there is.

A long, dark shadow, not defined properly, as if not quite *tuned in.*

"Joshua!"

Finally, he stops prattling on and whirls around. I hear him catch his breath.

"Aha. All right." He edges toward the park fence. "You chase it across. I'll head it off round the far side." He chucks me the resonator and, surprised, I catch it.

"Okay." I look down at it. "What the heck do I do with this?"

"Just follow the display. It's easy. And — Miranda?"

"Yes?"

"Don't take any unnecessary risks. That thing is *dangerous.*"

So this is it. We're hunting our enemy, tracking it down to its lair.

Breaking through shadows.

I'm keeping my eyes fixed on the space behind the swing, fixed on that long, dark Shape, and I've launched myself over the gate into Craghollow Park.

It's here, in the real world. In my room, in the Abbey, now here in the park. I haven't told Josh it's the same figure that haunts my dreams.

I'm aware of Josh, circling the edge of the park in the distance.

I step across the springy surface of the play area, duck under the jungle gym, and hover inside it, as if the domed steel cage is somehow going to give me protection. I have never felt more exposed in my life.

"Who are you?" I ask, my voice trembling. "What do you want?"

Cautiously I hold up the resonator. It's flashing, going wild. Scrambled numbers.

Then the digital readout goes blank.

I frown, stare at it. Something appears on the display.

Not numbers. Letters.

— *ashes* —

— *ashes* —

I'm recognizing what this is.

I duck out under the other side of the jungle gym.

Now, there is only open ground between me and the swings, and the shadows beyond them. I feel prickling on my forehead and under my arms. I can hear and feel my heart thudding through my body, and my mouth is sandpaper-dry.

— we —

— all —

I'm shaking so hard I can hardly hold the resonator. I'm trying to hold out for as long as I can. Get some readings. So that back at the Seaview we can plug this into the computer, and analyze it.

— fall —

For a second, a cloud passes across the sun, and the shadows around the playground change position.

I blink.

— down —

I feel something brush past my face. Searingly cold. Like a block of ice pressed to my flesh. I yelp and drop the resonator. I flip over on the muddy ground. I'm rolling over and over as if I'm falling down a hill, but the ground is flat.

The sky spins, fringed by trees — then I feel my hand being yanked and I am hauled to my feet to find Josh looking at me, concerned.

My breath is cold and ragged. My hair falls in front of my eyes and I shake my head. "Sorry," I say.

I rest my hands on my knees, and I scan the whole park.

There's a man walking his dog against the far fence, and two mums with toddlers wheeling strollers up to the play equipment. They're looking at me and Josh warily. Big kids, they're probably thinking. Look a bit weird and rough. Steer clear of them. I try to smile, but they look away.

Josh scoops up the resonator from where it has fallen beside the slide, slips it into his pocket, and smiles briefly at the two mums. "It's okay," he says to them, with his usual easy charm. "All yours."

"It just went," I say, hurrying after him as he strides off. "I didn't see where. And Josh . . ."

He stops, turns around. "What?"

"The rhyme — it was on the resonator."

He nods grimly. "It's trying to tell us something. Come on. Let's make ourselves scarce."

THE POD: SATURDAY 10:35

Slam!

Miss Bellini drops the heavy, leather-bound book open on the table, and we all stare down at it.

We're gathered around the wooden table in the Pod. My head still aches. I'm dosed up with the strongest over-the-counter medicine, but it doesn't seem to be doing any good.

Although my head is swimming, I try to focus on the book. The pages are mustard yellow, crinkly like autumn leaves, and thin as tracing paper. I remember Ollie saying Miss Bellini was going to get a book out of the British Library, but that seems ages ago.

Miss Bellini spreads her hands, smiles.

"I just wondered," she says, "if any of you, while glued to the Internet and your mobile phones, ever considered that the answers might lie somewhere more obvious?"

"So what is this?" asks Josh languidly, pointing at the book.

Miss Bellini peers over her silver glasses, sighs. "It's a *book*. A collection of sheets of paper or parchment, printed with ink, bound together in a durable material such as leather or cloth. They were very popular from the Middle Ages until, ooh, at least about five years ago. Commonly found in *libraries*. Remember those?"

"Ooh, miss, miss!" says Josh, raising his hand mockingly. "I know, miss. The things the government wants to close in case we start reading books and asking useful questions."

Miss Bellini smiles indulgently.

"Sarcasm's the lowest form of wit, Joshua," Cal points out.

"But the most fun," offers Josh with a grin.

"Hmm. Maybe," purrs Cal.

I glower at her, still smarting a little from our uncomfortable conversation yesterday afternoon. It kept me awake. Does Cal know more about me than she is letting on? I wonder what it was she wanted to say to me but couldn't.

Miss Bellini sighs. "To answer your question more fully, Josh, this is one of the existing copies of what's known as the Constantinople Rubric."

"Try saying *that* with a mouthful of bubble gum," says Ollie. I smile weakly at his joke. "Sorry," he mutters. "Didn't know I said that out loud."

Lyssa giggles, but Miss Bellini frowns sternly.

"A very old book," Miss Bellini goes on, "and a very *rare* book. I've had to have a special pass issued to remove it for seventy-two hours from the British Library's Dangerous Book Archives."

"That . . . doesn't really exist," I say.

"Oh, and you *know* that, do you, Miranda? Of course it exists. It's in a fortified titanium vault underneath St. Pancras station. Your Shadow-card grants you access, but for on-site research only. With protective gear on. Remember that. You may need it one day."

"I've been there," says Ollie. "It's cool. They've got the missing five Shakespeare plays, the unexpurgated King James Bible, and the scripts for the unmade *Star Wars* movies."

"And the first version of *Wuthering Heights*," says Lyssa, shaking her head. "Very odd. You should see all the stuff she took out."

"So," says Miss Bellini, "the question is, what do we have here? What is this force? What's our *evidence?*"

"Extreme temperatures," says Lyssa, her hand in the air as if she's at school. "Exchange of heat and cold. Toasty to frosty."

"It likes energy," I say, anxious to make a contribution. "Plus this thing's got a weird obsession with the 'Ring Around the Rosie' rhyme from the time of the Plague."

"It looks like . . ." Josh pauses, gnawing his fingernail, and everyone turns toward him. "Okay. We stood there and faced . . .

something in the Abbey. And in the park. And yet . . ."

"And yet," I say, picking up on what he's getting at, *"we can't picture exactly what it looks like."*

I close my eyes.

I see a darkness, a shimmering column of blackness like something trying to tune itself into reality . . . I see a shape with many faces, with pale, smooth skin and with gnarled, yellow pustules, too . . . with frightened child-eyes but the brittle teeth of an ancient crone.

And I see the child with long, dark hair, running across the field, the trees burning in the distance . . .

"A master of disguise?" says Ollie.

"Or mistress," Cal counters frostily.

"Miranda?" says Miss Bellini's voice, and it sounds deep and resonant, echoing both in my head and in some dreamlike cavern. "Can you see it now?"

Without even looking, I can sense the shadows gathering around me in the Pod. I can feel them. I close my eyes so tightly they hurt. I can feel my temples throbbing. I'm remembering the trick with the hemispheres and the ball, and how I thought, how I *felt*, my way to the right answer. It's all about not doing things the way you feel you should, not thinking in a straight line the way your mind screams at you to, but stopping thinking, letting your mind wander, feeling in tune with your body and allowing your instincts to flow. . . .

"Yes," I say.

My eyes snap open.

"It's a shadow," I say. "A dark, long shadow. Hooded, maybe, like a . . . like a monk. No, not a monk . . . it's female, definitely female. It's . . . a woman. A girl. Outlined in bright fire. Sometimes there's burning . . . a forest, on fire. The sound of horses. Maybe soldiers? And there's a strong smell, like . . . like . . . death."

"My uncle did a barbecue like that once," says Josh.

Miss Bellini holds up a hand, shakes her head at him with a frown. It's obvious that his flippancy is tolerated only up to a point.

And it haunts my dreams. Like it wants something.

I look into Miss Bellini's eyes. For a second, they scare me.

"A girl, then?" says Miss Bellini.

I nod. "A girl, a woman . . . all these images merging into one. Lots of different women. A young girl, a pale-looking woman, a wrinkled old granny, all at the same time." I shudder. "And she . . . her skin . . . she looks like a Plague victim."

"Do they all seem like the same face?" asks Lyssa curiously.

"That's just it. They are . . . and yet they're not. It's so hard to explain."

For a few moments, there is silence in the Pod. They all look at each other, as if I have confirmed something.

"I'm sorry," I say softly. "This . . . thing, it's been haunting my dreams. I didn't dare tell everyone the full truth. Sometimes I don't know if I am asleep or awake. I don't fully understand what's happening yet."

Then Miss Bellini breathes out, leans back, and calmly turns the pages of the Constantinople Rubric.

"Very well," she says. "A fiend in female guise, possibly able to change its appearance, wandering the earth, feeding on raw energy wherever it can find it, perhaps weakening. And yet never straying far from this immediate area . . ." She looks up sharply. "So why here? Why *now*? What's *changed* in Firecroft Bay over the last few weeks?"

"Maybe it likes fish-and-chips," says Josh.

Cal gives him a languid smile.

Miss Bellini is leafing through the book, her eyes flicking back and forth. For a few seconds, there is no sound in the room except the rustle of the pages and our own breathing.

"A shape in the form of a young woman," says Miss Bellini softly, "although appearing more often in the form of a barely distinguishable shadow. Gaining strength through the absorption of heat as it attempts to stabilize its physical form." Her finger jabs down on the page. "*Animus*," she says softly.

"Annie-what?" I say.

"Animus!" says Miss Bellini sternly. She goes over to the Whiteboard, and with a thick red marker she writes the word.

ANIMUS

We all stare at it.

"Linked to the Greek *anemos*," she says, "meaning air, wind, or breath. According to the Rubric, a name given to a bodiless life force, a dark form of spiritual energy. It has no actual fixed physical form of its own . . . but it moves from host to host. Every few decades — or centuries, depending on how long it can keep the body alive — it takes a new form."

"What happens each time the host dies?" Ollie asks.

Miss Bellini reads on. "When a host is lost, the Animus has a certain amount of time to renew itself . . . needing to absorb vast quantities of energy in order to do so. The problem is, the psychic link might not stabilize, in which case it will revert to its previous, dying body, leaving the new host in an emaciated state . . . and then it moves on to another, and another, and another. . . ." Miss Bellini clears her throat. "Like shedding a used carapace."

"Do we think there's any kind of . . . rational explanation?" I ask. "One that isn't supernatural?"

"Ah, well, we tend not to work like that," says Cal. "It saves time if you just assume from the start that anything is possible."

I hate this turbulence inside me. All these contradictions and confusions. I feel as though I'm running away from my own shadows.

Miss Bellini continues. "So, listen, guys. Our Animus. For now, it's bodiless. It's like a malevolent spirit existing outside the physical realm. But as it gains power, it can mimic the human form and use it for its own ends."

There's a silence in the Pod for a moment.

"A new form," says Cal softly. "So it's looking to make a psychic connection and emerge into the physical world. It's attached itself to someone. It's *become* someone. Or it's *becoming* someone . . .

or *they're* becoming it." She shudders. I'm surprised. I'm so used to seeing her taking things in her stride.

"Mimicking the human form?" I say nervously. "You mean, like . . . disguised as a person?"

"A full, convincing representation of humanity," says Miss Bellini. "But one that continually needs . . . replenishing. Topping-up, if you like, through intake of energy. Until it can stabilize . . . and finally *take over that form altogether*. The consequences of that would be disastrous. Incalculable."

"What do you mean, Miss Bellini?" asks Lyssa timidly.

Behind her glasses, Miss Bellini closes her eyes. "At the moment," she says, "this thing exists in a form that is not fully physical, not fully human. It's attempting to form a link, a bond, fixing on this place, this time, on a particular person it needs as a host. Why this place? I think we all know that. The Convergence is strong, and all the dark history of Firecroft Bay only enhances it." Her eyes snap open, and she looks at each of us in turn as she speaks. "Miranda's visions have helped us enormously. Without her we would not have been able to put the pieces together. But we have. We can."

I smile. "I'm . . . glad I could be useful," I say carefully.

"Indeed," says Miss Bellini, and she gives me a warm smile. "We must be very, very careful here. My inclination would have been, perhaps, to allow this thing access to the physical world and defeat it there . . . but . . ."

We all wait to hear what she has to say. The silence seems to crackle in the room.

"The Plague," says Miss Bellini. "The Black Death. Do you know how many people it killed?"

"Around a hundred million," says Josh quietly.

Everyone looks at him.

"I've been doing my research," he says, shrugging.

Miss Bellini nods. "Josh is correct. Almost the same as the entire population of modern-day Mexico, if you want a comparison. And almost twice the current population of the United Kingdom. We have no way of knowing how something like that would have mutated . . . how it would resist modern-day medicine. We could be looking at a pandemic. And this thing, this . . . Animus . . . it doesn't care. Maybe it was human once, but now . . . all it wants is survival. It doesn't care about me, or you, or your mums and dads and brothers and sisters. It doesn't care what it would unleash on the human race."

I think of Truffle, nuzzling against Mum's shoulder, and I go cold.

We look at one another now, and for the first time, I think, we all realize that we are dealing with something vitally important here.

Not just for Firecroft Bay, but possibly for the whole of this world.

CHAPTER THIRTEEN

hunting

THE OLD VICARAGE GARDEN: SATURDAY 20:03

Backward . . . and forward. Backward . . . and forward.

When we moved in and I saw the Old Vicarage had an old wooden swing, I never imagined I'd actually use it.

I used to play on swings a lot in London — we were always going to playgrounds when I was little. Dad would pull me up as high as he dared, and I'd be screaming in delight, giggling, ready to be launched into the air, and then I'd feel him let me go and I'd go zooming off, like flying into space, making a huge arc in the air, feeling the rush of the wind on my face as I kicked and pushed to keep it going higher and the seat almost disappeared from under me. . . .

I'm swinging quite gently today by comparison. Mum's having a work meeting in the house, and Tash is looking after Truffle.

Backward . . . and forward. Backward . . . and forward.

It's all going to happen, now.

It's all coming to an end.

We just need to make sure it is the end we need, and not a disaster. I shiver when I think of the responsibility.

I'm thinking about that conversation I had with Josh on the beach, after we had been in the café.

* * *

I remember standing there, the salty wind in my hair, and Josh's smile as he turned away and started to walk back across the pebbles to the steps leading up to the Esplanade. His long, dark coat flapping in the sea breeze, and his hair blowing across his face . . . mocking, twinkling eyes . . .

There's something really odd about all this, something that's been bothering me all for a while. Like our enemy knows us and is just playing with us, teasing us. Trying to see how far we will go and, each time, taking it a step further. As if it somehow knows in advance what we've been thinking. The bus, the computers, the Abbey, the park . . .

I dismiss the thought. I don't like it.

I jump off the swing and land on all fours, like a cat, on the muddy grass. For a moment I crouch there in the fading light and just listen. Saturday evening. It always feels like a time when something should happen. Like a time when the world breathes out after a hectic week and a busy weekend of soccer or shopping or homework.

That feeling again. Of being observed.

Only this time, I am.

Jade's leaning against the back garden gate, arms folded, shades on even though the sun is setting.

"All right?" she says.

I straighten up, a bit embarrassed at having been caught jumping off the swing like a little kid.

"I didn't know if you were . . . talking to me," I say nervously.

She shrugs and makes a noncommittal noise.

"Look," I go on, "I'm sorry about . . . about Thursday. On the pier. And thanks for helping me yesterday. You were right, I needed to get home. I felt like . . . like death warmed up."

"I've just . . . been walking round," she says softly. "I think I might . . ." She sighs. "I don't think I'm gonna fit in round here, Miranda."

Mixed emotions rush through me. A sense of panic and loss, even though I haven't lost anything yet. "What do you mean? Is this about the pier?" The evening gloom seems to have become deeper and more threatening, and there is a chill in the air. "I didn't . . . Look, I'm still not quite sure what I'm . . . doing with all this."

She holds both hands up. "I'm not gonna stop you being friends with the Weirdos, Miranda. Ain't up to me, is it? Nah, it's . . . There are things in this town I don't like. It feels a bit creepy sometimes. Shadows, and that."

I try not to react. "All seaside towns are a bit weird," I manage.

"Hey," says Jade, "look . . . you remember when you first came? When we went round the arcades eating chips? We ought to . . . you know, do that again."

"Yes. Yes, let's." I nod and smile eagerly, but I can tell Jade doesn't mean now.

"I might be going away for a bit," she says. "That's why I was standing on the pier. Thinking. Trying to size the place up. Decide if it's worth sticking round."

I fix on the first thing she said. "Away? How? Have you got anywhere to go?"

"There's my grandma in Basildon. I don't really know her, but, well . . . she wouldn't mind me dropping in for a bit. I've got a sleeping bag."

I'm worried about her now. "Okay, but . . . Jade, don't just vanish without telling anyone. People would worry. I'd worry. And that Mrs. Armitage, she seems . . . Well, she might be a bit fearsome, but it does seem like she cares."

Jade shrugs, hands in pockets. "Yeah. Maybe."

I'm getting the sense that she is holding something back. "You're not just going to take off, are you? I mean, look, I know you can handle yourself and all that, but people . . . you know . . . people get into trouble."

She gives a half smile. "Like I said, I need to work out if it's worth sticking around."

"What you need is to finish school or you'll never get a job."

She laughs. "You sound like old Armitage."

I feel myself blushing. "Sorry. But it's true."

"Lots of things . . . *could* make it worth sticking around," she says carefully, and she takes her sunglasses off now. Shocked, I can see that her eyes are red-rimmed, as if she's been crying. "Like . . . like if I knew I had a really good friend who'd be into the same stuff as me, and who'd stand by me whatever, and who wouldn't let nothing come between us."

I'm still trying to shake this weird, fluey headache. I'm really hoping Jade isn't going to ask me to do anything tomorrow. That's awful, I know.

"Does this have anything to do with Ryan Crofts?" I ask hopefully.

She makes a face. "Who?"

"Ryan Crofts. You were telling me about him yesterday, before I went home. That he might want to go out with you."

She shakes her head, looks away, leaning against the gate in that casual, worldly way of hers.

"There ain't no Ryan Crofts," she says coldly.

"What?"

"There's no bloody Ryan Crofts, all right? I made him up!"

"Okay, okay! Keep your voice down." I glance nervously toward the house. I don't want Mum coming out and getting involved with this. "You . . . *made up* a boy?"

"Yeah," says Jade, and she gives her head a little shake, maybe at herself or at me. "I made him up to make myself feel better."

"But why? There must be tons of guys who like you."

"Oh, you *think*?" She sounds so furious I almost take a step back. "It was just . . . one more thing, Miranda. One more thing to try and make myself think I wasn't unhappy here, okay?"

I don't know how to feel now. I want to hug her. Two weeks ago,

I would have, but now I feel too awkward. "I'm sorry. Please . . . don't go anywhere. You'll be in school on Monday, won't you?"

She smiles, shrugs again.

I look at my watch. "I've got to go in," I say guiltily. "Look . . . come and say hi to my mum."

"Nah, not tonight, babe." She nods, puts her shades back on again. "Thanks for the chat. I feel a bit better. Ciao."

And before I can even properly wave good-bye, she is through the gate, heading off down the road toward the shore, not looking back. I watch her getting smaller in the twilight, a slim, dark figure with a cloud of hair, framed against the pale beach and the red sunset clouds.

It feels odd, watching her go, as if it might be the last time I see Jade Verdicchio. I want to call out, run after her — but she has already disappeared into the distance.

Everybody seems to be having these conversations with me where they half say stuff, and expect me to fill in the gaps. They must all think I'm really good at it. I don't like to tell them that I'm struggling in the shadows.

SEAVIEW HOTEL: SUNDAY 10:49

I get an urgent call to come in on Sunday morning.

That's weird. Unexpected. I grab some aspirin, try to believe my flu, or whatever it is, has gone, and run past Mum and Truffle, barely giving an explanation of where I am going. I grab my skateboard, bomb it down the Esplanade to the Seaview Hotel. When I get there, they are all already clustered around the computers in the Datacore.

Ollie's hands flicker across the keyboard and the rest of us stand watching.

"Lyssa and I have been trying to trace energy surges in the area similar to those we are getting now," he says. "We cross-checked some data with the records from those old disks."

Lyssa holds up a sheaf of papers. "Most of them turned out not to be suspicious. Although we did find one account of a weird fire at Brooke Manor. No known cause, three people killed, police files left open."

"And?" I say.

Lyssa shrugs. "Problem is, it was in 1881."

"I don't get it," I say. "How is that relevant?"

Miss Bellini, swiveling on her chair, holds a hand up. "Bear with us, Miranda. I think you'll find this . . . interesting."

There is something about the way she says *interesting* that I find quite chilling, as if it isn't going to be a good kind of interesting.

"Okay," I say uncertainly.

"Altogether, I found three examples," says Ollie, "of clusters of unexplained energy drains or surges in the area." He clicks the mouse, and the big workstation screen above him splits into three. "First — the fire at the Manor."

He brings a picture up on the screen — it must be a very early photograph, showing the gutted interior of the manor house with charred beams poking out like bones at odd angles and blackened grass on the lawns.

"Then there was this, from 1924."

Ollie clicks the mouse again, and a picture appears in the central screen that makes me catch my breath and lean forward. It's an old car, with those funny-looking raised headlights. But there's something odd about it. It looks pale, washed-out, and the windshields have cracked.

"That," says Ollie proudly, "is a Citroën B2 from the early twenties. Top car. Or at least it was, before it was subjected to a temperature of around minus 100 degrees Celsius." Ollie looks up at me, almost apologetic. "Got reported in the papers at the time. Caused a stir, and soon forgotten."

"Like these things often are," Lyssa points out. "They put it down to freak weather conditions."

I look in amazement at Josh, Cal, and Miss Bellini. "Then that's . . . Did you *know* about this?"

Josh clears his throat, not able to look me in the eye. "Hear the rest of it, Miranda."

How does he know all this? He was with me yesterday, chasing that thing across the estate and the park. They must have been having secret text updates.

"And finally this one," says Ollie, and clicks a third time. Another picture zooms into place on the far-right screen, this time a large, square, white building with red lettering on the front. "I'll just magnify this," says Ollie, and the picture zooms in on the name: "EMPIRE."

"The Empire Ballroom," says Josh. "My grandmother's always talking about that. It's where she and my granddad met."

Ollie nods. "It was knocked down in 1972 to make way for the new Odeon cinema. But before that, one night in March 1969, the whole place was suddenly drained of electricity — heat and light disappeared from the ballroom as if someone had just sucked them out. Made the local news. Again, they found perfectly good explanations: faulty wiring, rapid power loss in the generator, and so on." Ollie spins around in his chair, spreading his hands. "Three incidents, decades apart. And I bet these weren't the only ones."

"That's it, then," says Cal. "We're sure."

Sure? Sure of what?

Miss Bellini looks at Josh, and raises her eyebrows as if to say "your call." Josh looks at Cal, who shrugs.

There's definitely something going on here. They're all exchanging such *shifty* looks. Ollie's got his arms folded. Lyssa's looking down at the desk. For some reason none of them will meet my gaze.

"Show her the rest," says Cal softly. She is sitting half in shadow, sipping coffee. Her voice sounds almost sad.

Ollie sighs, flexes his fingers. "Okay," he says. "Josh checked the parish records and electoral rolls for these dates, just to see if anything odd turned up."

Josh nods. "I'd been looking up the links with the Plague. History of the Crag Hollows and so on. So I already had it all to hand."

"Then," Ollie goes on, "I got some nifty software to cross-check with some photo sources. One that turned up again and again was school records."

"School records?" I get a prickle on the back of my neck. For some reason, I don't like the way this is going.

A black-and-white picture of a group of Victorian children zooms into view on the left-hand side of the screen — girls in lace bonnets and boys in caps and waistcoats. "1881," says Ollie, moving the cursor over each of them in turn. The next, also black and-white, shows children in smart suits and lace collars, looking a little further on in time. "And 1924," says Ollie. And then finally, on the right, a more modern, color one — a bunch of kids in cardigans and V-neck sweaters, the girls with styled-looking hair and the boys with bad pudding-bowl cuts. "And that's 1969. All archive photos of local primary schools from the library database."

I shrug. "And?"

He makes the first picture bigger, zooming in on one girl's face in the Victorian group. It looks blurred, but Ollie does something with the mouse and suddenly the features are sharper.

She's dark-haired, with big, dark eyes and a wide mouth.

There's something weirdly familiar about her.

Then he does the same with the nineteen twenties group, zooming in on just one girl, and finally the same again with the class from the nineteen sixties. Each time he cleans up the picture so that it's sharp.

I step forward and peer at each of the three pictures in turn.

The clothes and hairstyles are different, of course, but the girls all have the same features — glossy dark hair, dark eyes, sharp face, that cheeky wide mouth.

"Gran, mum, and daughter?" I ask.

Miss Bellini comes over and gently puts a hand on my shoulder.

"Not quite," she says. "Look again, Miranda."

I do so. And now I feel my heart rate quickening and my hands growing prickly and hot and damp with sweat.

Because I've seen it.

No.

It *can't* be.

"Do they look familiar, Miranda?" asks Miss Bellini.

I nod dumbly. The room seems to be wobbling.

"So they should," says Miss Bellini quietly. "All three of these girls have exactly the same face."

She raises her eyes, and for a second her glasses are full of soft, blue light.

I stare at Miss Bellini, trying to focus. And when I look at the three images again I know what she is going to say. I almost don't dare hear it, and yet I know I have to.

Miss Bellini says: "It's the face of your friend, Jade Verdicchio."

CHAPTER FOURTEEN

giada

My eyes are blurring with tears.

I'm hurrying along the marina, past the expensive shops and the moored boats. This is only a few minutes from the Seaview, but it's the posh end of Firecroft Bay, the bit they did up when they forgot about the Esplanade and left the Seaview to rot. Seagulls shriek above, as if they are laughing at me.

I find my way to the end of a jetty and stand there, arms folded, my tears blurring the sea and the masts and the breakwater in my vision.

There's a cold wind here, zipping across the masts of the boats and ruffling the awnings of the little trinket shops and fishing-tackle places. I huddle into my jacket. It's a good one: strong, sturdy black leather with loads of zip pockets like a motorcyclist's jacket. I remember when I chose it from the shop. Just after Dad died. It was too big for me then, too baggy and too teenage, and I thought Mum was going to tell me not to be stupid as it was so expensive. And yet she bought it for me.

He'd have liked it. *You look cool, Panda,* he'd have said.

And here I am now, leaning on a rail in Firecroft Bay Marina, and both the jacket and the memories are keeping me warm. An ordinary girl in a biker jacket, jeans, and Converse, hair tangling in the cold wind. Nobody would give me a second glance. And yet I know too many things about the world now. Things I wish I didn't.

My head is spinning with thoughts of Jade. I don't know if I have been deceived, or if that conversation last night was supposed to be telling me something more than I picked up. This is happening to me a lot. Why has she gone away? I'm starting to feel more angry than afraid, angry that I don't know what's going on.

I sense him behind me. I don't need to turn around.

"I . . . didn't know," says Josh softly.

"Go away." I'm amazed I don't say something ruder.

He sighs. "Fine. You know what, Miranda, I'm fed up with doing this."

I half turn toward him. "Doing what?"

"Buoying you up. Chivvying you along. I know you're new, but I thought you'd have come good by now."

He pauses, comes to lean on the rail beside me — not looking at me, but staring out to sea like I am.

"I *like* you," he says. "I mean, you're annoying, and you prattle on too much, and someone ought to tell you that the Avril Lavigne look went out years ago, but . . . But yeah, despite it all, I like you, Miranda. I thought we worked well together. But there are times when you have to put doubt aside and just face the truth. However uncomfortable it may be."

"Easy for you to say."

For a few seconds neither of us says anything. Then he says, "Maybe this isn't for you, Miranda. Because if you're going to let personal feelings get in the way —"

I round on him and face him, squaring up to him — and he actually takes a step backward. Wow.

"Personal feelings? Is that what you call it? Jade is my *friend*, Josh. And now you're trying to tell me she's this . . . *thing* we've been looking for all along?"

"Well," he says, scratching his ear. "I'd go for 'neo-vampiric embodiment of a dark spiritual life force,' myself, but I suppose *thing* will do if you can't come up with bett —"

"Don't get *clever* with me!" I step toward him and he actually backs away again. "I don't understand. You told me it wasn't her. Ollie did, on the pier. We . . . There . . . She's not —" I break off, feeling my eyes prickle with tears. My throat is raw and angry.

Josh shrugs. "The data . . . wasn't complete," he says apologetically.

I'm so angry with him, I almost shove him.

He lifts his hands up. "Okay, okay. Look . . ." His eyes narrow. "Seriously, Miranda. You've seen the evidence. Three times, three faces. *The same girl.* And it makes perfect sense."

"I don't believe it."

"You know it. We all know it. She's the Animus. She's hundreds of years old, Miranda. She's the thing we're looking for. The thing that could kill everyone. She's the 'Ring Around the Rosie' girl.

175

And she's been running rings around *you* all right."

"You can talk," I retort. "All this time you thought she was a Mundane."

"Well, yes. Hmm. Bit of a misjudgment there." Josh pulls out his phone, checking messages. "Anyway — we know where she is. Target lockdown initiates in five minutes." He raises his eyebrows at me and grins. "It's endgame. Are you coming or not?"

Josh, Miss Bellini, and the others, always knowing more than me. Haunted abbeys, shadows, intrigue, and betrayal. Life on the edge of reality.

I don't want to go on.

I don't need this anymore.

"You know what, Josh?" I say. "I'm not." I lift my chin defiantly, feeling the cold salty air on my face. "You go. Because . . . because I'm finished."

He looks vaguely surprised. "Oh. Okay." He turns, as if to go. "You're sure about this?"

I nod, feeling both weary and relieved. "Yes."

"All right," he says. He puts his hand out. "All the best, then, Miranda. We won't bother you anymore. No hard feelings."

I look at his hand like it's a dead fish.

"Customary gesture?" he says.

I give him a reluctant smile and shake his hand. "Okay, Josh."

"That's my girl," he says with a smile.

And he slams his other hand onto the back of mine, so that he has me caught in a double-handshake.

For two seconds, I can't move my hand from his grip.

Josh pulls away from me.

"I'm really sorry," he says.

I look down.

There is something on the back of my hand.

It looks like a flat pink disk. And there's *cold* spreading out from it, hitting my veins, rushing through my body.

I gawk at my hand in horror, and reach to try and pull the disk off, but I can hardly move my other arm. I feel all woozy. This is what I imagine being drunk is like. My legs suddenly lose the power to support me, and my knees start to buckle.

Josh grabs me before I hit the pavement.

"Steady," he says softly. "Don't hurt yourself."

"Wha' . . . you *done?*"

"It's a simple skin-pad tranquilizer. Just a standard Level One."

"*What?*" I stare at the disk on my hand, trying to focus. My entire body feels like it's shutting down for instant sleep, and my limbs are going numb.

"Hits the nervous system and gets flushed out in hours. Don't worry. It's harmless. Mutant form of a flunitrazepam derivative. You'll be okay."

"Flu-what?" I say in horror, my own voice echoing in my head.

The sound of the sea, swirling like weird static on the radio . . .

Blood rushing . . . The seagulls screeching . . .

Josh's face, blurring now . . .

Ollie, taking me into his confidence about his sister . . .

JumpJets blasting out from Jade's laptop, the latest video on YouTube. "Give what you can, and I'll take the rest/Do your worst, baby, 'cos I know you're the best . . ." The electronic drums throb and pound in my head.

The Shape on the beach . . .

The girl running from the blazing forest, smoke wreathing her as she turns away from me . . .

The crone in the Abbey . . .

Long, dark hair hiding their faces . . .

I keep trying to focus as I feel myself slipping away.

"We can't have you warning Jade," he says. "I'm sorry."

I try to move my mouth.

I get as far as "You —"

And then my legs give way, and everything goes black.

SOMEWHERE: SOMETIME

She's pointing at me.

I'm boarding it along the seafront, trying to get away, wheels whizzing fast. I kick the tail and go into a jump-spin.

No, I'm running now, and the pebbles are going kssh-kssh-kssh under my feet. I can hear the sea washing in my mind, and yet, for some reason, I can't turn my head to look at it.

The seascape shimmers, fades. I am on the edge of the blackened field again, under a reddening sky. The smoke hangs over the burning forest and the smell of sulfur is strong and pungent.

I can hear bells, deep and loud as if they're sounding the doom of the world.

And the girl is running through the misty smoke, running toward me, arms spread wide, hair spread out and wrapping itself around her face as she runs.

Ring around the rosie.

Her face is hidden, but now she comes to a halt a few yards from me. I stop, breathing hard, my eyes heavy.

"What do you want?" I say. "What do you want?"

Soft, tinkling laughter echoes in my mind.

And now her voice, singing the song that day in the tree in the garden of the children's home, where she seemed so kind and so carefree.

A pocket full of posies.

I'm walking up to her. My feet leaden, as they were in the Abbey that time. Everything is mixed now: bells and sea and fire. I can hear the sound of the seagulls as if on a tape loop, as if mingled with the singing of the nursery rhyme.

Ashes, ashes, we all fall down.

I take several steps forward and suddenly I am there. I am there. I reach out, trying to pull back the veil of hair.

Her face is —

* * *

I sit up, screaming.

"It's okay, it's okay."

Someone's voice. I don't know whose. I am hot, breathing quickly. My heart is hammering, and I can feel the vibrations of an engine all around me. I take a few seconds to focus my eyes and my mind.

I look frantically from side to side, trying to work out where I am.

"Miranda . . . ? Miranda? You with us?"

It's Josh. He comes into focus. He has his hand under my chin, almost affectionately, peering into my eyes. He nods, and Lyssa — yes, she's there, too — hands him a slim flashlight.

I can hear a voice saying, "She was there. She was there," over and over again, and I suddenly realize it's mine.

"Eyes open wide," says Josh, and peers into my eyes, shining the flashlight into them one by one. Then he nods, toward the front of the vehicle. "Equal and reactive," he says. "She's back with us."

I realize I am in the VW camper van, and Miss Bellini is up in the front, driving, with Cal in the passenger seat. Cal turns, her red hair loose, and gives me a reassuring grin. That's weird. Lyssa and Josh are on the folded-down backseat with me, and Ollie is down on the floor with all the computer equipment and other junk that Miss Bellini carts around.

"What happened?!"

My voice sounds croaky, and only now is my heart rate slowing to something like normal. Josh passes me a bottle of water and I gulp from it gratefully. When your mouth is that dry, water tastes like the sweetest stuff on earth. I feel it sloshing down my chin. I cough and splutter as I swig too much down at once.

Josh slaps me between the shoulder blades

"Had to get you back with some adrenaline," he says apologetically. "I was stuck with dragging you back to HQ. Lucky it was only just across the road."

I realize there is a small, absorbent white patch on my upper right arm, and it stings a bit. *"Adrenaline?"* I say quietly.

Josh nods. "Got you up and running again. Ready to go?" he says, clapping me on the shoulder.

I shrug him off. "No. No, I'm not! How *dare* you mess about with me like I'm some sort of . . . vivisection experiment. What gives you people the *right?*"

The camper van judders to a sudden halt. Miss Bellini turns around in the seat, and with one hand still on the wheel and the other draped across the back of the driver's seat, she gives me an apologetic smile. "No right at all," she says. "But needs must. I'm really sorry, Miranda. We'll try not to do it again."

"How am I going to explain this to my mother? She'll think I've been doing drugs."

"An emergency rubella inoculation," says Miss Bellini. "I've already arranged for a letter to go out."

"German measles?" I scoff. "I've already had that one." (And she never wrote me that note about getting out of gym, did she?)

"It's a mutant strain," says Cal, leaning around. "Don't worry, you'll be covered."

Miss Bellini nods. "Fighting fit?" she says.

I scowl again. "You don't trust me, do you? Any of you? Just

181

because I'm friends with her. With Jade."

"We need you to be on board for this, Miranda," says Miss Bellini sternly. "We need to contain this, and we need to contain it *now*. Before it brings an apocalypse."

I feel a creeping horror. I remember Jade's face. On the pier, narrowing her eyes at me. In school, when I felt ill, taking me under the arm and leading me to the nurse's. In the tree house. My friend. Getting close to me, and all that time —

No. It can't be.

I look out of the window.

I gather my resolve. I made a decision a while ago to be part of this, to trust them and let them in. They are not the Weirdos; they are my friends. I need to go with this, I need to be sure about this. If this is the truth . . .

I thought I knew who I could trust. But I think of all those times when Jade tried to steer me away from the so-called Weirdos, and I feel angry now that I might have been used, betrayed.

I nod. "Let's go in."

MILLENNIUM ESTATE: SUNDAY 13:01

We have stopped on the other side of the street from the Copper Beeches Children's Home.

It's chilly. Wind rustles the leaves and scatters the blossoms like snow. We line up, a row of silhouettes — Josh and Cal in their long, dark coats, me in my leather jacket, Ollie in his duffle coat.

Lyssa is staying in the van with Miss B to monitor readings.

All of us have our eyes screened with wraparound shades. There is a good reason for this. The thing uses heat and light, we know that much, and these are fitted with ultrascreen lenses to protect against flares and flashes. Miss Bellini doesn't want us taking chances. It seems we've reached the point where this thing could attack us if cornered. If Miss Bellini's worried, I am.

"Anything, Miranda?" says Josh.

"I'm trying to get a . . . sense here. There's nothing."

"She could be screening," Josh murmurs. "Okay. Cal, how are we doing this?"

Cal sounds cool and confident, as usual. "You and Miranda take the front. Get in on some pretext. Ollie and I will scout around the back. Bound to be a window or a cellar or something we can get in through."

My heart is pumping again, but this time it's good. This time it's not fear, but a sense of purpose. I take another gulp from the bottle of water, as my mouth still feels like sandpaper.

"Okay," says Josh. "Let's do this."

He and I start up the driveway to the door, while Cal and Ollie duck down so they are screened by the hedges and bushes as they make their way around the edge of the building toward the back.

Josh and I march along without speaking, our footsteps crunching on the gravel. We walk up the steps to the front door.

"We've not got a cover story yet," he says worriedly, reaching out his hand for the door knocker.

I grab his hand and pull it back. "Who needs cover stories?"

I flip out my library card, just as I did when I first got into the Seaview Hotel by foul means. Josh watches with interest as I slip the plastic card into the tiny crack between the wooden door and its frame, at about the height where I estimate the catch to be. I wiggle it up and down a few times, putting my ear and hand to the door.

Josh is looking around nervously. "Whatever you're doing, could I suggest you get on with it?"

I smile. It's nice getting one up on Josh for a change. "Patience is a virtue, Joshua," I murmur. I like that. It's something my mother often says. I'm not in the habit of quoting my mother, but it can be quite useful.

There is a *click*, and the door opens.

"Not bad."

"That's praise from you."

He nods. "Keep behind me."

"But —"

"You do as I say!" His voice is suddenly harsh, his eyes cold and full of determination. He really means this. He means it more than anything. "I'm not putting you in danger."

I shrug. "Her room's on the first floor," I say. "In case you wanted to know."

Josh nods again. "Right." He enters the hall and I follow, keeping close behind him.

I'm feeling great now, like the water and fresh air have cleared

184

out my head. I'm ready to go. Ready for anything. I feel decisive, resolute. As if Jade's deception and betrayal have given me new strength.

Mrs. Armitage doesn't seem to be around, luckily — she's probably in the kitchen at the end of the hall. As quietly as we can, Josh and I start to climb the stairs.

Halfway up I grab his arm. "What are we going to do when we find her?"

He looks down at me, raising his eyebrows. "You don't know?" he says, and that cheeky half grin is back.

"No, or I wouldn't be asking!"

We reach the top. Josh holds my gaze for a second, but he doesn't answer the question.

"Which one is it?" he asks, looking down the landing.

I nod toward the purple door facing us at the corner of the landing, the one with the huge JumpJets poster and the soccer pennants. "That one."

"Okay."

He starts to stride forward, but I grab him and pull him back, almost managing to spin him around to face me. I'm surprised at my own strength.

"Joshua!" I'm hissing at him through clenched teeth. "Tell me what is going to happen here."

He hesitates, then takes out a small, slim yellow cylinder about the size of a glue stick.

I frown. "And what's that?"

"Insurance," he says, and there's something unsettling about the way he says it.

As he turns and heads down the corridor to Jade's room, I see him slot the cylinder into a gleaming silver device he's unfolded from his pocket. It extends like a collapsible tube. A kind of gun. My eyes widen.

In the same instant, I hear the fire door open down the corridor and I see Cal and Ollie running toward us. Cal's boots are pounding on the wooden floor.

"Do it and get out now!" Cal shouts. "We're detected!"

Josh looks back at me, once.

The unmistakable voice of Mrs. Armitage echoes through the house.

"You kids! What are you *playing* at?"

Josh steps forward and kicks Jade's door open. It swings, hits the wall with a loud slam, and springs back, but Josh is in.

And now I realize things have gone wrong, and I've got to stop him. Nobody has thought about me. They've just presented me with this situation. Told me that my friend is not who I think she is. It feels wrong now; it feels as if we are doing something we should not be. What gives us the right? It's Jade. My first real friend here.

I scream in anger and throw myself at the door, knocking Josh off-balance. He staggers as he swivels around in a half circle, leveling the device.

He stops. We are all breathing heavily. It takes us a second or two to realize that Jade's room is empty.

The sash window is open, curtains fluttering in the breeze.

Ollie hurries over to it, leans out, shaking his head as he looks back at Cal. "There's a drainpipe," he says.

I allow myself a small smile. So. Jade is not stupid. She really has upped and gone, just like she said. But where, though? Where would she have gone? She mentioned a grandma in Basildon, but . . .

Cal curses and kicks the wall, dislodging a small amount of plaster.

"Careful," I say. "You'll have to pay for that."

Cal spins around and comes storming over to me.

I've done it now. That wasn't a good idea.

She shoves me hard, practically pinning me up against the wall. I swear I have never seen her green eyes so cold and hard with anger.

"You *stupid* little . . . You could have got us all killed!"

My head is pounding. I don't like the way Cal is snarling, gripping my collar. I can feel my throat constricting in fear. Cal's hot, minty breath is right up in my face. And I don't know if it's the fear, or that latent psychic ability I'm supposed to have, but the two fillings in my teeth are *humming*, aching.

Like I said. Dangerous wildcat. And I'm cornered now.

"Leave her," says Josh quietly. "It's not her fault."

She doesn't look at him, but keeps her cat eyes on me. "If it had been in there . . . think what could have happened. All because *she* can't focus. I told Miss Bellini. I said she'd be no good."

I'm shocked, and I look from Cal to Ollie and then to Josh.

Josh looks abashed. The silver gunlike device in his hand seems incongruous. "We had to vote on whether we thought you'd be an asset to the team. We all voted yes, except . . ."

Cal backs away from me, letting me go. The strange feeling in my teeth starts to ebb away.

"Yeah," she says with a shrug. "Except me." She doesn't look sorry.

"We all made mistakes when we started," says Ollie. The others turn to look at him. "Well, it's true."

Cal opens her mouth, I assume to give a cutting retort. But there is then a thumping on the stairs, and we all turn as one.

Mrs. Armitage, red-faced and puffing, is heading up the landing toward us. She does a double take when she catches sight of me.

"Miranda! Could you *please* kindly explain what all this is about?"

I look back into the room, where Josh is somewhat sheepishly trying to hide the large, silver, gunlike object behind his back, and failing. I turn back to Mrs. Armitage.

"I'm sorry, Mrs. Armitage," I say. "Just stupid kids. Having fun."

I push past her and head down the stairs, not looking back.

Not at her, nor at any of them.

CHAPTER FIFTEEN

lockdown

THE POD: SUNDAY 14:55

"I am *so* not doing this!"

I am angry. Miss Bellini sits calmly, tapping her pen on the desk as she listens to me. Josh may be trying to look nonchalant — his feet on the table like he hasn't got a care in the world — but he's clearly upset. He's not such a tough one after all.

The others are below us, a thirty-foot steel ladder away, and I bet they've been able to hear me shouting for the last few minutes.

"What are we *doing*? It's a Sunday afternoon. Ordinary kids, oh, yeah, 'Mundanes,' right," — I do the sarcastic air quote thing — "they're out at soccer, the movies. What are we up to? Chasing around after *nothing*. A shadow that doesn't exist. Running around on a wild-goose chase after one of my *friends*, actually."

Miss Bellini puts down her pen as if she's irritated by her own tapping. "Miranda," she says calmly, in that velvety voice of hers. She seems to be gathering her thoughts. "Miranda . . . I am starting to wonder about you."

I stop in my tracks. "You are?" Crossly, I push a strand of hair back out of my eyes.

She smiles. "Yes. I'm thinking I made an even better decision than I thought in taking you on. Sit down."

"I'm standing. I want to be standing up when I hand you this back." I pull out the black Shadow-card and fling it onto the desk.

Miss Bellini nods, presses her fingertips together. "Joshua," she says, peering over her glasses, "perhaps you'd like to explain to Miranda about the hardware?"

Josh holds up the silver device. "It's a, um, well it's a psychotronic wave inverter," he says. "Sorry. Think of it as a sort of . . . spook gun."

I fold my arms. "Now you are *seriously* winding me up."

"It's . . . what we use when there doesn't seem to be any other resort," says Josh. "It tunes into the sub-ether, um, wavelengths, and homes in on paranormal activity. And then if it can lock onto the essence" — he taps the yellow cylinder — "it traps the beast. In here. Like a fly in amber."

I snort. "So what happened to circles of salt? And chalking a pentagram on the floor, and muttering 'flibberty-dibbety-dob, begone, foul fiend'?"

Miss Bellini sighs. "Don't *mock*, Miranda. The old ways, the old rituals of banishment, still have their uses, but . . ." She spreads her hands, raises her eyebrows. "There are new ways of doing things. We're finding our feet in the technological age."

"Anyway," Josh interjects, "I think circles of salt are for slugs." Miss Bellini and I glare at him. He shrugs. "Sorry. Just . . . you know. In the interests of accuracy."

I lift the device up off the table. It's surprisingly light, and I can hold it in one hand. Gingerly, I put it back on the table.

"It's all right," says Josh, "it's not going to explode. Just needs . . . sensitive handling."

What annoys me is the way they let out their knowledge a bit at a time, as if they still don't trust me to know everything that's going on.

And Cal — predatory, slinky, feline Cal. I had wondered if I might start to trust her more, but she has shown her true colors now.

I start to think about some of the conversations that have gone on in Control — or on the secret phone frequencies — when I haven't been around.

Like Cal voting against me.

What other secrets does she keep . . . ?

"Miranda," says Miss Bellini, "you have to realize what we are *dealing* with." She leans forward, and her dark face looks grim. "This . . . thing you know as your friend Jade Verdicchio is old and cunning. Centuries old. It is a devious and malevolent force. One of which most of the people you walk past every day are blissfully ignorant. But we . . . we have a *duty* to sort this out. Because nobody else is going to."

I nod. "Yes, Miss Bellini. I know." I slump into a chair, feeling a crashing tiredness in my legs and arms. I haven't slept much in the past couple of days. "I keep seeing things that make me question . . . everything I've always assumed. It's just that it's all so *new* to me."

She smiles. "It was new to me once, Miranda. But I need to know you are with us. I need to know we can count on you." She fixes me with her hard gaze, dark eyes compelling me to look at her.

"You can count on me, Miss Bellini."

"You're Jade's friend, we know that. If there is anything — anything at all — that you're holding back, something that might help us . . ."

Basildon. That's Essex, isn't it? Other side of London. Two hours away or more. I wonder what her grandma's name is. If it's her dad's mum, then . . . well, there can't be that many Verdicchios in Basildon.

I hesitate.

"I'll tell you if there is, Miss Bellini."

Why did I do that? I don't know. Something isn't right, that's why. Something hasn't quite convinced me. The way they are treating me, the way Cal reacted especially, makes me want to keep that piece of information for myself, as something that may be useful.

Miss Bellini holds my gaze for a second or two.

"All right, Miranda," she says softly.

There is a clattering on the ladder, and the others join us, Cal with an armful of rolled-up paper.

"Just a quick thought," Cal says, and unrolls what turns out to be a detailed map of Firecroft Bay and the harbor. "Josh, talk us through this."

"Oh, yeah. These old maps. I got them out of the archives. Been trying to map where the ley lines converge . . . to see where our errant Animus might end up." He looks up at me, with a charming smile, trying to draw me back in. "You in with this, Miranda?"

I shrug.

"Okay," Cal says. She gives me a warning look. "Where did you see it in the park?"

I point, grudgingly, to the south corner of Craghollow Park. Lyssa leans over and puts an X there with a red marker pen.

"And then it drew energy from the school and the area around it." Lyssa draws a ring around our school.

"And the Abbey."

Lyssa draws another red ring.

I think I'm starting to see where this may be going. I look at Josh, wondering if he's had the same thought, but I can't read him.

"The power drains we've been scanning for weeks," Lyssa says. She marks three more red crosses on the map, all on or around the Millennium Estate. We stare at the map, at the crosses that are now forming a circle.

"Anything linking them?" I ask.

Cal looks up, smiling. It's almost as if she has forgotten her earlier anger with me. "Yes, actually. Lyssa?"

Lyssa marks one more cross on the map — on a large building, right in the middle of the circle of crosses.

"The power station," I say.

"They supply the green energy for Bartram Buses as well," says

Ollie. "The company that does the school run."

"Places with Plague connections, too," says Josh. "The Crag Hollows, where they burned witches, and the Abbey, where victims were buried . . ."

"It's all coming together," I say.

Josh whistles softly. "You know," he says, looking up at me, "this psychic stuff is all very well. But at times, you just can't beat old-fashioned detective work."

"Yeah," says Lyssa cheekily. "We don't all get to play with the toys."

Josh grins, picks up the spook zapper, and points it playfully at Cal. "Get thee hence to endless night," he says.

"Don't. Even as a joke." Cal pushes him away. "Miss B, tell him."

"Joshua," Miss Bellini says softly.

"Sorry."

"But when?" I say suddenly.

Everyone turns to look at me.

I shrug. "It's all very well knowing the likely where," I point out. "But we can't stake the place out every night and hope. And from what you lot tell me, I gather the police aren't much help to you in these situations. So when's it going to happen?" I look around at them all. "Well? Anyone got any ideas? Because I have."

Miss Bellini, to her credit, does no more than raise an eyebrow. "Do share, Miranda," she says. "But first . . ." She pushes my Shadow-card back across the table toward me. "I take it you won't be resigning *just* yet?"

I hold the card between my thumb and forefinger for a few seconds.

"Not yet," I say, and pop it back inside the pocket of my jacket. "So. Who wants to hear my theory?"

They all look at one another, then back at me.

"But before I tell you," I say, "I want no more lies. No more half-truths. No more not telling me how you deal with things, and *no* more stupid secret tranquilizers!"

I glower at Josh. He holds his hands up defensively. "That wasn't my idea," he says in a pained voice, and glares at Cal. She looks away.

O-kaaaaay. *That's* noted. Thank you, Josh.

"You stop doubting me," I say. "From now on, I'm in on *everything*. Got that?"

Surprisingly, nobody laughs.

I think they know I really mean it.

DATACORE: SUNDAY 15:15

We cluster around the main computer desk. Ollie is at the keyboard.

"You'd better be right about this, Miranda," says Cal.

"Tell you what, Cal — if I'm not, then you can kick me off the team, okay? And I'll go back to being a nice little Mundane, eating chips, playing netball, and not getting in anyone's way. That suit you?" I smile sweetly.

"Girls!" says Miss Bellini firmly.

We exchange sharp looks and return our attention to the computer.

"What's up?" Lyssa is leaning over Ollie's shoulder.

"Nothing." He's jabbing at keys and clicking the mouse, opening one window after another. "Just some glitch in the software. Something's got into Image-Ination, I think. I'm dealing with it."

"I thought we were properly firewalled," says Miss Bellini sternly.

Lyssa shrugs. "Well, they get cleverer all the time."

"Okay, here we are. Sorted." Ollie has brought up some information on the screen. Looks like a restricted-access website. I don't know how he did it, but I'm impressed. "There we go," he says. "The new centralized power grid for the whole of the Southern Central England region . . . switches online at midnight . . . *Tonight!* Wow. Miranda, you're right."

I try not to look smug. "Don't sound so surprised. There was a mention in the paper the other day. I just put two and two together. So, it takes over the power grid . . . what does that mean?"

Ollie looks up. "Well, the power station's been built. It's all automated and it's ready to go online. When it does, thousands of millions of computerized electrical circuits will be focused on one central register, and the energy will spike. All the power will flow from there, probably in a web formation."

"And our friend," murmurs Josh, "will be the spider."

Cal has been standing on the other side of the room, strangely silent through all this. But now her eyes are glistening. "So we have to stop it," she says. "Her. Whatever. We need to get there now." She looks at Miss Bellini. "Miss?"

I still don't know what shady connections with the authorities Miss Bellini has, but she seems to be able to pull strings when she wants to. We're not an official organization, though — the government doesn't even like to admit we exist, from what she's told me. So maybe it's all done discreetly, in brown envelopes on street corners. Or perhaps she's got incriminating stuff on a minister or two. I think it's best for us not to ask, frankly.

Miss Bellini looks up and smiles. "I'll get the necessary . . . procedures taken care of," she says.

THE POWER STATION: SUNDAY 23:16

The VW camper van is parked at the entrance. We are ascending the steps, spread out in a line with Miss Bellini leading.

We were all up for getting here earlier, but Miss Bellini had to get the place cleared of staff and have our entry authorized.

The main part of the building looks like a huge steel drum, the size of a soccer stadium, gleaming in the moonlight. There are chimneys stretching up, like giant guards, and at the front there's a jumble of steel and glass admin blocks that look as if they've been stuck on at random, with a wide flight of stone steps leading up to the glass entrance doors.

I feel important, but also frightened. I've got a denim satchel over my shoulder, shoved full of a few odds and ends I picked up from HQ — you never know when they're going to come in useful. I've been trying to suppress the thudding in my head and ignore the odd noises and shadows around me. I'm not sure I'm succeeding.

"Where are the staff?" I ask, puzzled by the darkness of the place and the empty parking lot below us.

"The staff have gone off for some very convenient fire-safety training." She gestures through the glass doors as they swish open for us. "So we've got just one security guy, and one big computer network."

When we enter the lobby, we see it is lit by a mellow orange light from glowing disks in the ceiling that cast long wobbling shadows. There's a dark shape behind the desk. My heart skips a beat, but then I see it's the security man, dressed in a blue uniform with a badge saying "RAY." He gets to his feet as we come in.

"Can I help you, ma'am?" he asks, looking at Miss Bellini with a certain amount of respect, and then down at us with a questioning expression.

Miss Bellini flips her official government pass at him. "Anna Bellini, special operations. I want this entire facility taken into lockdown immediately." She hands the security man a sheaf of bound papers. "You'll see I have full authorization."

I feel sorry for Ray. Bet he thought he was going to have a quiet night in, maybe make some tea and listen to the radio. He flips through Miss Bellini's documents, shining a flashlight on them.

"I wasn't told," he says.

Miss Bellini flashes him a quick, tight smile. "Maybe they

didn't think you were important enough?" she suggests.

He glowers at her and picks up the phone. "I'll have to check."

"I'd be disappointed if you didn't." Miss Bellini takes her gloves off. She looks around. "Something the matter here tonight?"

Ray shrugs. "One of those power drains again. The computer's got the backups running here, but most of the building's on standby."

"I thought it looked dark," I murmur, looking up out of the glass window on the far side, gazing up at the dark steel drum of the power station itself.

"Yeah," says Ray as he waits for the phone. "You don't wanna be going up there."

"Oh, we're quite prepared, thanks," says Miss Bellini with a smile. "You, ah, may as well take the rest of the night off," she adds to Ray.

He looks dubious. "Can't do that, ma'am. More than my job's worth." He nods. "I'll be in the back room with my coffee if you need me." He shuffles off, muttering.

"Splendid," says Miss Bellini with a taut smile. "Lyssa, Ollie . . . get the equipment set up." They nod, and hurry off to the table in the lobby, to get out the computer equipment and other bits of scientific paraphernalia. Miss Bellini nods at me, Cal, and Josh. "And you three — we're going upstairs."

I feel a thrill of danger, anticipation, terror. "We are?" I say. "But . . ."

Miss Bellini has produced four candles in brass holders from her bag, and hands them out to me, Cal, and Josh, keeping one herself.

"Not flashlights?" Josh asks in surprise.

"The Animus can drain electrical power," she reminds us curtly — and, striking a match, she lights the candles in one smart, swift movement.

"If that thing tries to get in," murmurs Josh, looking up at the high ceilings, "we'll know about it."

He swings down the bulky canvas bag he's brought with him and puts it on the nearest seat with a *thump*.

"Uh-uh." Cal indicates the readouts on the resonator, which she's been waving about. "And I swept the entire building for pyro-electric traces as we came in. Nobody here except us chickens." She grins. "I've always wanted to say that."

I can't help smiling, too.

Lyssa and Ollie are crouched down beside the desk, with a complex collection of equipment next to them. It looks like a heap of junk — two old laptops, some microphones, and a radio all lashed together with multicolored spaghetti wiring and duct tape, and linked with crocodile clips to a — to a — what is that?

"What's the thing with the little screen that does the wobbly green lines?" I ask Lyssa, nodding at it.

"It's an oscilloscope," she says.

Of course. How could I forget?

"That . . . mess is a bit low-tech, isn't it?" I ask. "Did you build it?"

She smiles at Ollie. "Geek Boy did."

"Blimey." I'm impressed. "Sorry I called it a mess."

Miss Bellini has come over. "Anything?" she asks.

Lyssa shakes her head. "Not a thing."

Miss Bellini sighs and looks at her watch, then looks down at me. "This had better not turn out to be a wild-goose chase."

I have had no communication at all from Jade. I'm starting to wonder if she has disappeared from the face of the earth.

Or from this reality.

Something is really, really niggling at me about this whole thing, though.

I can see that's what my brain does sometimes. Gets a deep, dark sense that something's wrong. Mixes thoughts and dreams and instincts. Like it sent me a message and told me to get out of the way of a speeding truck. Helped me look beyond the dark figure in the park to see the form of a girl . . .

But its face . . . Its face . . .

The fleeting worry . . .

Leaving Ollie and Lyssa in the foyer, Cal, Josh, Miss Bellini, and I head farther inside the building. Into the darkness.

There's no emergency lighting here — only the glow of our candles. There is an odor of smoke and hot wax over the chemical new plastic smell of the place, and the shadows dance. I'm looking over my shoulder every second.

There's a vast central atrium with a marble floor, escalators straight ahead, flanked by a waterfall, and a big central glass column with a brass elevator. There's also a metallic spiral staircase. It's trying to look modern and old-fashioned at the same time.

I crane my neck, lifting the candle upward. Miss Bellini risks shining an electric flashlight for a second, and we can see the atrium goes all the way up to the top of the building. On the various floors, fronds of red creeper hang over gleaming chrome balconies.

"Come on," says Miss Bellini, "the energy spike is programmed for midnight. We need to be right at the top of the building."

Candles aloft, we start to ascend the stairs. Miss Bellini goes first, and indicates that I should follow. Josh is behind me, and Cal brings up the rear. The flickering candlelight gives all of our faces an unearthly glow.

This is it. Whatever this is about, whatever the Animus really is, we are going to find out here.

CENTRAL POWER COMPLEX: SUNDAY 23:45

Far below us, the scattered lights of the town glitter like orange jewels. The rhythmic pulse of the lighthouse flashes across the bay, catching stormy waves in its beam. Some distant lights are moving slowly across the sea, probably a night ferry.

I know this is a special place. Out there, under the darkness, is England — beautiful, patchwork, ancient England, with its standing stones and its legends and its witches and warlocks. And here we are, twenty-first-century kids, trying to make sense of it all with our computers and iPhones and MP3 players.

Sometimes I get a twinge of terror about what would happen if the modern world just disappeared. If we all had to go back to roasting sheep over fires, sticks and mud, bashing rocks on stones. We'd cope with it far worse than any people from previous centuries. All those old skills are lost now. It's like time and progress are taking us forward too fast.

I turn away from the view and face into the room, holding my candle up to see as much as I can.

We're in an octagonal chamber with a window across two of its sides. A viewing platform with a railing runs all the way around it. In the sunken middle of the room is an octagonal arrangement of eight computers around a central pillar. At each apex of the octagon is a glass globe on a black pole, eight of them arranged like some modern imitation of a stone circle. These are linked to eight separate energy terminals, each supplying a different part of the South Coast. Miss Bellini is looking carefully at each of them, peering under them, making notes on a clipboard. High up in the ceiling, there is a red digital clock, counting hours, minutes, and seconds. It now reads **23:46:03**.

High up here, the winds howl and buffet the building; it's like being in some chilly, creaking old medieval castle. And whose domain is it?

Cal is just pacing up and down, texting, candle in one hand and phone in the other. Her red hair is gleaming in the candlelight.

Josh sidles up to me. "Okay?"

I nod, my face taut with tension.

Cal's phone beeps. We all jump.

She glances up at Miss Bellini and at Josh, and nods to each of them. Not to me, I notice in annoyance.

"They've got something," she says. There is a pause. Then, "Really? Here . . . ? You'd better let her in."

My blood runs cold.

Let her in.

Someone has arrived and they are letting her in. What the heck is happening now?

And that's when it all starts to go crazy.

Cal puts her phone on speaker. "Ollie? Speak to us."

"Massive disturbance patterns!" Ollie is saying. "It has to be right on top of you!"

My blood turns cold at the way he says it. This is bad. Everything is happening at once.

I don't know if I am imagining it, but the room has started to turn darker. The orange light deepens until it is almost red, shadows lengthening further, as if we are all bathed in blood. There is a silence so deafening it seems to ring in our ears.

And then I can hear it.

Whispering voices. *Shush-shush-shush-asss-isss-hsss.* I can't make out the words, but the sound is clear enough. A female voice, chanting. It might possibly even be in Latin. Chanting. It sends chills through my blood and makes me feel weak as if . . . as if time and darkness are working together to drain the energy out of me . . .

I try to focus.

I look around at the others. "Can anyone make out what it's saying?"

They don't immediately answer. Josh and Cal look at each other in alarm.

"Can you hear it, Miranda?" says Miss Bellini gently.

"Yes. Clear as anything. I mean, I don't know what it's saying, but I can hear its voice." I look around at her in sudden realization. "Can't you?"

Miss Bellini shakes her head. For some reason, she has her cell phone out.

I look at Josh, and at Cal. "Can't *you* hear it?" I ask them.

Josh has lowered his head slightly, and looks not at me but across at Miss Bellini. "It isn't fair," he says. "We ought to stop this now."

Something shifts in the room, and I feel as if I am acting on a stage now. It all seems *wrong*, artificial.

And then my whole body goes bitterly cold and burning hot, both at the same time. And my brain kicks into action.

I am standing in the shadows, in the center of the room, staring at my friends. I don't understand what's going on.

Josh looks embarrassed. Miss Bellini looks uneasy. But Cal — she has that cool, threatening confidence she's always had. She unfurls herself from the wall where she's been leaning and starts to stride around the room, never taking her eyes off me.

"I didn't . . . quite tell you the truth earlier, Miranda," says Cal quietly. "In fact, a lot of us haven't been telling you the truth for quite a while." She looks at Miss Bellini for the nod of approval — and gets it.

I'm feeling a sense of panic now. "What is it? What do you mean?"

"We've let this charade continue for just one reason," says Cal. "To let the Animus think it had won, then we could pin it down and contain it."

"Charade? What do you mean?"

"You asked me if it was already here. And I said no. And maybe that was the right answer, in one sense. But in another, well, maybe I should have said yes. Shouldn't I?"

She looks down at me from the railing, her green eyes so bright they are almost burning into me.

"In fact," she says, "it's been with us for quite a while. Anticipating our moves. Enjoying teasing us as it waited for the right moment."

What does she mean?

Her pale face looks triumphant.

"How has it known, Miranda?" she says softly. "How has the Animus kept one step ahead?"

I back away, my hand over my mouth.

"You see, this Animus is very *clever,*" says Cal. "It's had to learn to adapt, to survive. It can exist in all kinds of different wavelengths, outside the physical world. We know that — we've seen that. It sort of tries to tune itself in. It can even live inside data — it can *corrupt* data."

"It . . . can?" I ask weakly.

206

"Oh, yes. It can change the nature of a computer program, for example. Manipulate the results so that they look totally misleading. It's playing with the people who are trying to hunt it down. Toying with them. *Laughing* at them."

"All right, Cal," snaps Josh. "That's enough."

"Oh, no," Cal says. "It's not *enough*. She needs to know. But I think she already does, on one level."

Shaking and shivering and burning up, I stare at Cal. Behind her, the clock reads **23:48:07**.

Time ticking away to midnight.

"You," I say. "It's not Jade, it's *you*."

I look desperately at Josh for help. He's impassive. Miss Bellini, too.

Cal opens her mouth wide and laughs, *laughs*, as if I have told her the funniest joke. "Don't be so stupid," she says.

Josh steps in. "Miranda," he says. "You have to realize. This is very difficult for you, but . . . we came to realize that the Animus — the Shape — whatever you call it . . . had established a psychic hold on someone in Firecroft Bay. That it was in female form, and that *something* here was giving it strength, giving it life."

Behind them, I can see something happening.

There is someone coming up in the elevator.

The green numbers above the doors, from 1 to 20, are lighting up one by one. It is on 3 and rising steadily.

"Go on," I say slowly.

I can hear my pulse throbbing in my ears.

Like a warning. Like a danger sign.

Ba-boom. Ba-boom. Every strand, every thread is coming together, here, now, in this room here at the top of this building.

The elevator's now on 4 . . . 5 . . . 6 . . . I wonder if Josh, Cal, or Miss Bellini have noticed.

Josh says, "I asked myself the question — what's changed here in the last few weeks? And then I asked — wherever this thing's been seen gaining a hold in the physical world, wherever it's been strongest, what's been the common link?"

Ba-boom. Ba-boom.

"This place," I say. "Obviously. Renewable energy source. That's why we're here. It feeds off electrical power. Right?"

Above the elevator, the floor numbers steadily climb.

8 . . . 9 . . .

"Yes," says Josh. "But there's another thing. The one element that's always been common to it, the one thing that's always followed it around, the one key, unwavering factor that has always seemed to be there, bridging the gap for this thing. The psychic link. The gateway. *Someone who had only just arrived here.*"

11 . . . 12 . . .

Josh looks unblinkingly at me. Sadly.

And it is as if I am being told something I have never known, and yet, somehow, have always known; it is like that illusion where, if you stare at it for long enough, you see either an old crone or a young woman, or both. Or like those Magic Eye books, where a three-dimensional image springs out at you, both there and not there, reaching into the real world and molding itself out of the air.

14 . . . 15 . . .

"You, Miranda May," says Josh. "It's you. It was always you."

The thing. The Shape. The Animus.

It's me.

My enemy is me.

CHAPTER SIXTEEN

flashpoint

WHERE AM I? I AM PARTLY HERE, IN THE POWER station, and partly on the seafront.

I can hear the screeching gulls and the crash of the waves as I walk, in slow motion, dragged down by my heavy legs. My bleary eyes struggle to focus as I stare at it.

There. A long, dark cloak, fluttering like a flag across the backdrop of a slate-gray sea. Reality shifts and twists, and it is standing in front of the blazing forest again, the smoke painting the blue sky black. I can smell the smoke — angry, pungent, sooty, and sulfuric.

The Shape does not move. But it's more than a shimmering column. It's a figure, hooded. Closer and closer I go, until I am standing facing it.

You saved me, I say in my head. *On the road in front of the café.*

The Shape looks up.

The long, dark hair frames a pale face, just as it did in the vision. Only now, she doesn't have the yellow skin and the angry pustules. Her face is moon-white, and her pale eyes glow with an unearthly light. Her mouth is a broad red stripe, and it is *smiling.*

"I almost have you," she murmurs. "Almost."

. . .

I am kneeling on the floor of the power complex.

"I've been afraid," I hear myself sobbing. "Afraid even to sleep. It comes in the darkness. Comes in my dreams!"

"We know," says Miss Bellini softly.

And now Cal hits a button on her phone. I hear a *beep*, and a second later the eight globes in a ring all light up, crackling, blue. *Ghost light.* I remember from the Abbey. They form a ring of power, surrounding me, keeping me safe . . .

No. Of course not. Not safe.

Keeping me in.

The central pillar is glowing softly, too, and so are the computer screens.

"Just keep still, Miranda," says Miss Bellini. "We're going to help you. We're going to break it."

I am shaking. I can feel my body twisting, my back arching, as something forces me down.

I am lying on the floor, my arms spasming out of my control. I feel my mouth open, hear an unearthly screech echo from it. There is a strong, harsh, burning smell.

"Break it?" I hear myself croak, and I try to lift my head through my ragged, sweaty fringe. "How are you going to do that?"

18 . . . 19 . . . 20.

The elevator pings.

The doors start to rumble open.

A thin sliver of light emerges from between the doors, fanning out into an arc, then a dazzling square of brightness. A dark figure is framed in the elevator doorway. I am shaking and sweating with terror.

The light spills out into the room and I cry out loud.

The tall figure steps out from the elevator, dressed in a dark suit, soft hair around her shoulders, light glinting off her glasses. Miss Bellini, Cal, and Josh — they knew she was coming all along, of course they did — turn and look at her as she passes through into the room.

Of course.

It all makes sense now. What Cal said to Lyssa on the phone. *You'd better let her in.*

I look up. I stare up at her shoes, her swirling skirt, her jacket, the jangling bangles. I look up farther still and I see that familiar face and that smile, the mouth that has kissed my head and read me bedtime stories on four thousand, seven hundred nights.

"Miranda," says my mother, crouching down and taking my face in her cool hands. "Everything's going to be all right."

CENTRAL POWER COMPLEX: SUNDAY 23:51

The pillar, globes, and screens pulse gently in harmony.

It's here.

Almost without any fanfare, it has appeared inside the circle of globes. A tall, dark figure that flickers and changes — from old crone, to young woman, and then to the girl with the ravaged skin and mouth.

212

Slowly, the Shape and I circle one another. Watched by Cal, Josh, Miss Bellini.

My mother is also in the circle. She walks calmly next to the Animus, unafraid.

It shouldn't surprise me that my mother should be tuned into something like this. I've been so doubtful about her powers and her knowledge, but she knows what she is doing. So they have asked her to be here. And just how much does she know? After all — my gift came from somewhere.

The Animus is there, and yet not there. I can feel her, part of me and yet not me, as if she is a dark reflection in a deadly mirror, a black, shiny mirror into the depths of another dimension.

The Animus shimmers, trying to stabilize.

She is not ugly. In fact, she is quite beautiful. Her face seems ageless, her skin porcelain white and so paper-thin you can see the veins through it. Her eyes still have that unearthly glow, but I can see now that they were originally slate gray, almost blue. Her reddened lips are thin and taut like a bow, with lines around her mouth that have come from suffering rather than laughter.

The Animus gathers the cloak around her, and as she walks, she leaves traces behind her, like afterimages — as if she is not properly tuned into time. Her breathing is hoarse and ragged. It sounds amplified, almost metallic, as if it's being relayed through a microphone.

"Tell us who you are," says my mother gently. She has her

fingers splayed out as if she's touching the Animus, but she isn't. "Tell us why you are here."

I fear it less now that Mum is here. I still don't have much faith in the healing powers that she believes in, but somehow the fact that *she* does makes everything more bearable.

And yet the voice, when it comes, still grabs me and shakes me.

I can feel the reverberations, as if it's speaking through my own larynx. I look in panic at my mother, but she raises a gentle hand to calm me. The voice isn't agitated, but it is still harsh and horrible, as if it had been burned.

"I was born Katherine Mary Brampton, in a small Essex village in the year of the Peasants' Revolt. The year of Our Lord, thirteen hundred and eighty-one. I am something more, but I always remained Katherine."

"Tell us about your family," my mother says.

"My father died," says the voice, "after the Battle of Smithfield. My mother ten years later. Nobody cared, as some had already marked her as a witch. Nobody looked after me. *The witch's daughter.* Maybe a witch myself. I fled, into the forest. I scavenged, I hunted. Until one day, at the age of thirteen, I saw the pustules beginning to form on my skin."

I swallow hard. I don't know what to say.

"*Ring around the rosie,*" she hisses. "You understand now?"

I hear Josh say quietly, "The Plague. Yeah, we'd worked that out. A while back."

"I thought I was destined to *die.* All those centuries ago. There, in my filthy encampment. Just another girl with the Black Death. It was everywhere. All that rotting flesh. Bodies piled high, no time to bury them. Sulfur burning in the air. You could smell the fires from miles away. Death on the wind. And then, one day, at dawn — the riders came."

"Riders?" It is Miss Bellini who repeats this.

My mother glances at her. "Anna," she says, as if she's telling her to keep quiet.

But the Animus — Katherine — answers her. "Armored horsemen. Dark-skinned. Carrying flaming torches. To this day I do not know who they were. Mercenaries, maybe. But their intention was clear. To burn the forest, and everything in it. I awoke to the thunder of hooves, and before I could even properly flee, the first searing flames had started to engulf my encampment."

Burning the forest. The image seared into my half-sleeping, half-waking brain.

"But you didn't die," says my mother.

"The fire . . ." She pauses. "The fire swept *through* me. Scorching hell-heat burned me up. I was sure I would be meeting with the Devil, for I knew I was not a godly child. *I knew I was going to hell.*" Her eyes snap open. "But I ate up the fire. I had . . . become inhuman. Or maybe I always was inhuman. Who knows? They said my mother was a witch. Perhaps they were right. All I know is this: They burn witches, do they not? Well, I stood there in the midst of the inferno and I felt the fire burn itself out around me, and I smelled the smoke and breathed in the filthy charcoal of the ravaged trees and the scorched earth, *and I lived*. The fire gave me strength. I returned to the village, trailing smoke in my wake. My feet made black prints of ash on the ground."

A girl running from the blazing forest, smoke surrounding her like ghosts. The girl and the Shape, Katherine and the Animus, one and the same. The witch's daughter, the demon. All these names people give to things they cannot understand.

Pain and weakness push me down, forcing me onto the floor of the room. I cannot take much more. She is growing stronger.

She goes on. "People saw me and fled. One man tried to kill me with an axe. It went straight through me as if it were a passing breeze. . . . Do you have any idea how simple those peasants were? How easily manipulated by stories of hell, of fire and brimstone? They *believed* in the Devil back then. The Devil was real. And as far as they were concerned, I wasn't just a witch's daughter now. I was the Devil's Child."

I swallow hard, not knowing what to say. I'm shaking, feeling sick and cold and tired. She circles me, and I almost feel her body pulling mine along with it.

I am becoming her.

"So then," she continues, "after my first death, I could go where I wanted, do what I liked. And that was the way it stayed until now. Expelling the heat from my body when it became too much, and absorbing it again from elsewhere when needed." She pauses. "Call me the Devil's Child, call me fire demon, yes, call me *Animus* if you want. I can soak up the energy from a burning barn or an exploding car, absorb it, use it."

I glance at the clock. **23:53:11**. I can't take any more. They need to do something.

"I have had so many lives, so many names. I watched Byzantium fall to the Ottoman Turks. I saw the Boleyn girl lose her head. I witnessed the liberation of France and the breaking of the Berlin Wall. I have watched cities, monarchs, dynasties, and presidents rise and fall. I have been on this earth for over six hundred long years. This world is going to destroy itself soon — very soon. *There is a darkness coming.*"

"A darkness?" The hairs stand up on the back of my neck.

"One that even you will not be able to resist, child. I can sense it. It's deep, buried . . . but there is a darkness even in you."

I don't know what she means.

"Yes. A darkness coming. All must change. Adapt to survive. And now this part of my life is over and I need renewal. I need to gain a hold in the world and become totally physical again."

"We won't let you do it," says Miss Bellini calmly.

"And why not?"

"You know what will happen. With all the accumulated, focused energy, your physical body will become a receptacle for destruction, for plague. Miranda would just be the first. You'll need to continue to renew over and over again . . . scouring the country for someone with that psychic link as the body fails, just

217

as your last body failed. *How many would have to die, Katherine?"*

The Animus hisses like a serpent, rounding on her. "You think I care? You think I care for the people who abandoned me, left me to die, to burn?"

Miss Bellini is still calm. "You are *dead*, Katherine. Accept that. Everything has its time and yours has come. The people who let you die went into the ground themselves centuries ago. Don't let this become an act of vengeance."

I huddle into myself, looking from the Animus to Miss Bellini, and then up at my mother. She looks calm, beautiful, resolute.

"You are not taking her," she says. "You can't have her."

The Animus opens her eyes wide, as red light pulses from them. "But see," she whispers, "I already have."

Her eyes become orbs of white, sending out lashing tongues of energy that scorch everything they touch. They whip across the room, burning and melting and searing.

The Animus steps forward, arms out in a deadly embrace, ready to enclose me. To become me.

Gasping, I look up at the digital clock. The crimson figures read **23:54:56**. They're powering toward that computer-controlled energy spike at midnight, and nothing can stop them.

"I can feel the Machine grow," says the Animus softly. *"Let it begin."*

CHAPTER SEVENTEEN

darkness

THE MOON SHINES INTERMITTENTLY FROM BEHIND rushing, tattered clouds.

I'm in a playground at night. It smells of decay. Swings creak in the cold wind, and laughter, ghost-children's laughter, echoes across the cracked, weed-infested tarmac. The slides are rusting. It is like Craghollow Park — a dreamlike version of it. But is this a dream, or is it real?

Above me, dark specks swirl in a blue-black sky. They could be birds or bats, or ash from a bonfire. Digital clock figures appear in the sky, as if written by lasers.

23:55:17

The carousel creaks, turning, even though there is nobody on it.

No — she is on it. With her back to me, a hunched shadow. She turns, turns, the hooded face coming into view. She looks up at me, and I see her face in the moonlight.

She has the face of a hag.

Her skin is not glowing and porcelain white any longer — it is yellow, dusty, like the old paper of the Constantinople Rubric. Her nose is hooked and deep lines are scored across her face, cutting through flesh misshapen by boils and pustules. Her spotted brown hands are clawlike, with brittle nails and bulbous veins. Her teeth are like splinters of yellow bone. Her body shakes as if she finds it a great effort to stay sitting.

"You saw this several times," she says with a harsh, rattling whisper. "The form I have been reduced to."

I back slowly away. "Where are we? What is this place?"

"Our bodies are still where they were. But now, we are battling for your mind." A horrible smile creeps across her face. "The link — that's all I need now."

"No. I won't let you."

"But I am already too *strong* inside you, Miranda May. You are so special. It will take very little force of will now, for me to become you." She gets slowly to her feet.

23:56:10

"I'm not afraid of you," I say. A cold wind whips leaves across the path.

It is as if I haven't spoken.

"I have occupied your body," she hisses, "and now I will occupy your mind. Take my hand."

She moves toward me, holding out one claw, and I'm running, stumbling across the playground, through the cold wind and the flurries of leaves. Beneath the swirling ash, or bats, or birds. Beneath the dark, rushing clouds.

On a rope bridge, a familiar figure stands, dark coat blowing in the wind, hair tumbling across his eyes, hands firm on the ropes. Josh looks like an admiral at the stern of his ship.

"Don't let her win, Miranda!" he shouts. "Fight her! Break her, for us!"

I run to the swings, and she is there, swinging backward . . . and forward . . . Backward . . . and forward . . . Just like me. I stop, back slowly away.

Lyssa emerges from the shadows behind the swings, holding her oscilloscope. The lines are going crazy, casting green flickers across the ghostly playground.

"You're one of us now, Miranda. Stay with us!"

Ollie is beside her. "You've got to be strong!" he says firmly. "I lost Bex. I don't want you going, too."

And on top of the monkey bars is Cal, her hair fire-bright in the moonlight. "Never give an enemy a reason to rejoice, Miranda. We're all on your side. Concentrate. Concentrate hard!"

I fall to my knees.

The Animus is there in front of me. I scramble to the slide, manage to get up the steps, as if the height gives me some illusion of escape. But it just makes me feel more isolated, and now I am at the top of the slide, cold, shaking, waiting to come down, just as I used to when I was a little girl.

It's waiting for me at the bottom. One gnarled, papery hand outstretched.

I can feel it pulling on my mind, willing me to let go of the bar, to slide down into its embrace.

"You need something that's your own."

It's Josh's voice, soft and urgent. He's beside me on the platform.

"What?" I say desperately.

"We can't help you now. You need to find something the Animus can't possess. A thought, a memory, an emotion. Something that will weaken its hold on your mind and banish it as the energy process begins."

We both look up at the sky.

23:57:10

I don't have long.

Something the Animus cannot own. A thought that is pure. Something that's mine alone.

23:57:44

Her eyes are furnace-bright, the claw reaching out.

It's no good. The wind is icy now, as if the sea itself is blowing across from the bay into the playground. I can feel myself slipping. The temptation to give in is so strong.

23:58:01

I think of all the people who have come and gone, lived and died here. The sailors and smugglers, the witches and the Plague victims. I think of how little time we have in life, of how short our existence actually is and how much we need to do to make it worthwhile. For there is nothing beyond. I am *certain* of that. I know this little life is all I have.

And you know what? There's no way I'm going to lose it.

23:58:29

"I'm sorry," I whisper, my eyes closed. "I'm so sorry for you. But I'm not going to let you take me as well."

"Miranda." It's Josh's voice, again, more urgent, on the edge of my consciousness. "The energy spike."

And then I realize that there is one thing. There is something she can never have. Something that can only ever be mine.

I only need to think of him, and he appears.

23:59:21

I remember that day one year ago.

I'm standing by the grave, my eyes burning with tears. It's stupidly sunny, the shadows too crisp and the birds too loud. The undertakers in their long coats moving as if in slow motion, the great, shiny black cars stealing along the flat gray road. My hand opens as I drop the sandy earth from the little box onto his wooden coffin and the soil obscures his name on the plaque. Knowing that this is the last time I'll see the place where his body lies. Turning away, not sure if I should brush the earth from my hands, looking at the people in their dark suits framed against the hard blue sky . . .

But no. Don't think of that.

Think of him alive.

Further back still, in my special and sacred memory.

I am two years old and it is the first time I have gone down the slide on my own. It seems like a huge, terrifying slope of metal, a great run into the unknown.

23:59:44

"Come on, Panda, my love," his voice says softly. "Let go. Let go, and I'll catch you if you fall."

23:59:52

I look down, and there he is. I see the creases of his smile and the twinkle in his eyes and his outstretched arms at the foot of the slide.

"Dad," I say softly, my eyes stinging with tears. "Dad."

I can sense the Animus, her anger burning into my mind and my soul and my being, and I think, No.

You cannot have this. You cannot be me.

I do have something left to live for.

23:59:56

I let go of the bar above the slide.

And I fall, into blackness.

23:59:59

CHAPTER EIGHTEEN

00:00:00

TOTAL DARKNESS.

No. Eight points of light.

Glowing, growing, rushing toward me. Reality tuning itself back in. Strength returning to my body.

I hit the world again with a jolt, like someone being pulled out of a dark tunnel into sunlight.

I gasp great lungfuls of air. It's like waking up the morning after being ill and drinking beautiful, cold water.

And she is screaming as the power is turned back on her, on her own life.

Her focus has gone. I have rejected her. Repelled her.

The pillar in the center of the room glows cherry red, then orange, and all the computer screens begin to show endless strings of numbers and letters, before exploding in a blaze of sparks. Just like in the school. There is a strong smell of smoke and sulfur. One by one, the glass globes pop, too, shattering like lightbulbs. I scream, terrified, covering my face. Alarms sound, and sprinklers come on. Water pounds the floor like a hundred power showers, frothing on every surface, soaking me.

The Animus kicks and thrashes as the haze of energy breaks her hold, *drags* her essence away, pulling her out of bodily existence. With a final shriek, she snaps out of view as if she had never existed. All that is left of her is a small pile of ash.

I am curled up on the floor, gasping, bedraggled, hands in front of my eyes. The beckoning figure of my father's spirit is imprinted on my retina.

The red digital clock is counting on from midnight now. Onward, out of the darkness and into the light.

Smoke drifts through the room like sea fog.

I see Josh step forward and scoop up the pile of ash into one of those little yellow cylinders I first saw him use at the children's home. He screws the top on the cylinder, puts it into his pocket, and nods to Miss Bellini.

Then my mother runs forward and hugs me, and I sob angrily for a minute or two.

We just stand there for a bit. We don't have to move or say anything. And then, slowly, we look at one another and nod in understanding.

CHAPTER NINETEEN

aftermath

THE OLD VICARAGE: TUESDAY 15:37

"You all right to entertain yourself?" asks my mum. She has Truffle over her shoulder, his diaper reeking.

I hold my nose and nod, trying to eat my cereal with some dignity while ignoring my smelly little brother.

"Kerry's coming to look after Thomas. I've got some visits to do."

So it's Kerry, now? I wonder, briefly, what happened to Tash. Oh, well. These "helpers" come and go all the time.

"Fine," I say, with my nostrils still pinched.

"Honestly, Miranda. You were little once."

I decide not to answer that, but go on eating my cereal and watching Mundane TV as it flickers in the corner of the room. What's this one called? *Snog, Marry, Avoid My Toddler's Fat Ugly Dog,* or something? I can't wait to get out of here and back to my friends.

My mother's hand is gentle but firm on my shoulder.

"You were incredibly brave," she says. "More than any of the others would have been."

"You think so?"

"I know so."

"I didn't really know what I was doing."

"We can go to the doctor," she says. "If you like."

I shake my head. "Really. I don't need to."

She nods, as if accepting this. "Have you got homework?" she asks.

"Math. I've done it."

"Really?" She narrows her eyes. "Are you sure?"

I open my eyes wide, spoon halfway to my mouth. "Look in my bag if you don't believe me! Fifteen equations, all finished. Did them last night."

Okay, so Josh helped me to get them done more quickly with the aid of a cheat website. But they're done. And I don't need math to be a Shadow Breaker. As we are now officially called, according to Miss Bellini.

"All right," says my mother. "Just asking."

It's good I don't have to lie, because I think she'd probably know. It's easy on the phone, but not face-to-face.

"Still all right for bowling next weekend, then?" she says.

Bowling? Next weekend? I rack my brains, trying to remember if this is something I'm supposed to know about. I take a big gulp of tea to hide my confusion.

"Sure," I say. "Next weekend . . . yeah, 'course."

"It's all okay," she says softly. "Really, it is." She squats down, so her eyes are level with mine, and gives me her warmest smile.

"And now you don't have to lie to me anymore about where you are."

I nod, smile. "Mum?"

"Yes, my darling?"

"How long . . . how long had you known?"

"About the others?" she says. "Or the Animus?"

"Both."

She lowers her eyes for a second. "I knew there was a kind of darkness around you," she says. "It's my job to notice these things. But I didn't know what it was. Or how or when it would strike . . . and I was so worried about you. I felt so guilty."

"And Miss Bellini and the others?"

"I've known almost since you first got in with them." She smiles. "All those clubs you were supposedly going to. Not terribly convincing. What story do the others spin for their parents, I wonder?"

I've never thought about that. "I don't know."

"Anyway, I was torn, knowing you were putting yourself in danger, but at the same time . . . I knew that if anyone could help you overcome what was destroying you, it was Miss Bellini and her team. I had to let it happen. There are links at the highest level between Miss Bellini's contacts and the . . . well, let's say certain authorities I know. They have . . . networks."

This ought to surprise me, but for some reason it doesn't. "And you didn't say anything?" I ask.

"I didn't want to jeopardize it. It could have put you in more danger. And that's the way it'll stay. If you tell Miss Bellini you want to carry on, I won't interfere, I won't breathe down your neck. But you'll know I'm here if anything . . . disturbs you again."

I nod again. "Thanks, Mum."

"You know," she says, "I don't show it, but . . . I worry about you so much. I mean, it's enough that you're growing up and settling into a new place . . . But all this, too. I need you to be safe."

"I will be," I promise.

She touches my cheek again. "You're so important, Miranda," says my mother. "So important in so many ways."

I know she has said this to me before, not long ago. It seems like years, though. Her words seem to echo through time. But they are good words, and they reassure me.

* * *

It's all over, and the dust has settled.

Yesterday afternoon, Josh and I went out to the power station, but couldn't even get close. The place was sealed off — tape, mesh fences, armed guards in yellow vests with big, hungry-looking dogs, plastic sheeting over the shattered windows, the works.

We could see guys in camouflage gear and visored helmets going in and out of the building, carrying crates into army vans. They didn't even notice us as we stood and watched.

Couple of kids. We're kind of invisible, you see. Running in the shadows.

"Not our problem now," Miss Bellini said to us in the Physics lab at school. "The guys with the big boots come in and clean up.

It's what they do best. And for the moment, our electrical supply carries on just the way it has been."

I wonder about the papers, and the TV news, and the unofficial media like bloggers and so on. But nothing seems to have got out. That's the way the adult world works. Miss Bellini says that people like to be skeptical, but ultimately believe what they're told, and even those that won't at first usually do once they're given money.

* * *

Some nights, I lie awake thinking about the Shape. The Animus. Katherine Brampton the witch girl.

I think about the moment her shadow was broken, when the energy she should have absorbed to become me consumed her instead. I stopped her, kept her shadow at bay. I found the one thing that was mine and mine alone, that precious memory. And I clung onto it like a drowning girl clinging to driftwood as the storm raged around me.

Now, in my room, I'm thinking about the school photos we saw on the screen in the Seaview Hotel with the same face in all of them. She'd been clever. She used the Image-Ination software to morph the original girls into Jade, to throw us off the scent — just long enough for it all to work out her way. I should have realized when Ollie mentioned there was a bug in Image-Ination. Poor Jade. Just an ordinary girl caught up in it all, and she didn't even know. Good thing she took off to her grandma's when she did. Just lucky.

One thing bothers me still. One thing doesn't fit.

I heard the horses in some of my dreams, and then the Animus told us about them.

Armored horsemen. Dark-skinned. Carrying flaming torches. They burned the forest to get rid of the Plague. To scorch the Black Death from the land. Maybe. But who were they?

I know I'm not going to find out just yet. Something tells me I have seen a fragment of something more, a window to something deeper and darker, beyond this place and this time. More shadows searching for hosts, more shadows to break.

I'll need my new friends by my side.

SEAFRONT CAFÉ, ESPLANADE: SATURDAY 10:19

I spot Jade from the other side of the road, before I go in. She's sitting at the window table of the café, a Diet Coke in front of her. She's gazing out toward the sea, her nose ring glinting in the morning light. She hasn't clocked me yet.

This is the very place, I realize, where that truck almost hit me. A shiver runs through me. I cross the road carefully, just like they teach you. Looking both ways and listening all the time.

Yep, Cross at the Green. Good girl. Say what you like about me, but I don't make the same mistakes twice.

The doorbell jangles as I enter the café, and she smiles as she looks up and sees me. I go over to her and give her a big hug.

"So how have you been?" I ask.

She shrugs. "Oh, y'know. Not bad."

We sit down. "You ran away," I say quietly. "You didn't tell anyone where you were."

Jade grins. "I was only at my grandmother's. I'd hardly call that running away."

"Yeah," I admit. "As running away goes, it's on the poor side. Halfhearted, even. You're sticking around, then?"

"Yeah. I'm sticking around," she says. "I decided being bored here was better than being bored there."

"Copper Beeches taking you back?"

"For now," she says. "Old trout Armitage weren't too happy with me, but then, is she ever?"

"She doesn't seem easily pleased."

"Nah. So what 'bout you? What's been going on? Someone told me you was in a fire or something?" She narrows her eyes at me and takes a sip of her soda without looking away.

"No . . . not really. Well . . . I helped to . . . prevent an accident." I'm trying not to lie directly to Jade, without telling her stuff that would compromise me. "Look, it's difficult."

"Something to do with the Weirdos?" Jade holds her hands up. "It's okay. You don't need to tell me. I don't wanna know. Just as long as you've sometimes got time for your normal mates, I ain't bothered. All right?"

"All right," I say. "That's a deal, Jade."

"Want to come round tonight?" she says. "Some of the Beeches guys are ordering pizza, watching a DVD. We can all invite a friend."

"Yeah. Thanks, Jade. That'd be good."

I smile at the friend I almost didn't trust. The friend I was ready to think the worst of. I nearly gave her up. What kind of person does that make me?

I'm going to have to think about that one.

SEAVIEW HOTEL: SATURDAY 12:19

"Okay," I say. "This will need a bit of thought."

Josh sighs, folds his arms. "Take your time, Miranda. We're not going anywhere in the next few hours, after all."

I lean across the pool table, trying to peer right down the cue like Josh does, imagining the power I can get behind it.

"I mean," Josh goes on, "it's not like we've got anything better to do."

"Take it steady, Miranda," says Lyssa, watching from the side.

Cal is perched on a high stool, reading a book, but keeping an eye on the game. "The trick," she says, without looking up from her book, "is not to look too hard at the ball, or you end up hitting it off-center."

She's right. You look down the cue, and you look at the pocket, where it's going. Look at the ball and you don't angle it right. I tease the white ball with the cue, enjoying the smoothness of the wood across the bridge of my hand.

And then I bring it back, and fire the shot.

I've hit the white dead-on. I watch, not daring to breathe.

It powers across the table, bounces off the far cushion, comes back, still under a good momentum, and clicks with the red ball I

234

was aiming at — sending it rolling, rolling right to the edge of the pocket . . . teetering . . .

And it's in.

"*Oh, yessss!*" I punch the air. I spin around on my heel, pointing at Josh with my cue. "Bring it *on*, Pool Boy."

Cal snickers. Lyssa claps.

Josh looks annoyed, and doesn't meet my gaze. "Calm down, Miranda," he says. "It's just one shot."

"He's not a gracious loser, is he?" I say to the girls.

"Never," Lyssa says. "Although there is still a fifty-seven percent chance that he will win." I look at her, surprised. "Based on previous games," she says.

Well, okay. I have to bow to Lyssa's math. I shake my head and laugh, looking cautiously at Cal.

She smiles at me. I'm glad.

"Game's still on," says Josh caustically, as I'm stalking around the table and eyeing up my next shot. "There'll only be one loser here when we're done."

"Yep," I say, "and it'll be you."

From behind us, Miss Bellini coughs discreetly. "I hate to cut in at such an important moment," she says. "Miranda? Could I borrow you?" She beckons with one finger.

THE POD: SATURDAY 12:23

I slump into the leather swivel chair and put my feet up on the desk, folding my hands together. I smile at Miss Bellini.

"Quite comfy," I say. "You never know. In twenty-five years' time, Miss Bellini, I could be you."

She turns, peers at me over her glasses.

"I don't agree, Miranda," she says.

"No?" I can't hide the disappointment in my voice.

"No. I'd say fifteen years."

I grin. But she sounds very serious when she says it. Like she knows something I don't. Well, let's face it, Miss Bellini always knows stuff we don't.

Looking at the desk, I notice she has the three metallic hemispherical cups laid out again.

Noticing me looking at them, she gestures. "Remember? I think you may be able to do it now."

I remember when she performed the trick for me. Seems like ages ago. I swing my feet down, stare at the cups for a bit, and then start to move them about.

"Don't forget," says Miss Bellini softly as she sits down opposite me. "The speed of the hand deceives the eye." She produces the small white ball, seemingly from nowhere, and holds it up between her black-gloved thumb and forefinger.

I lift one of the cups and Miss Bellini carefully places the ball under it. I move the cups around, slowly at first, then more quickly. Miss Bellini is watching intently. I move them about for a minute, applying the gentle pressure of my fingers to the smooth surface of the cups.

Finally, I stop, leaving the cups in a perfect line. I gesture at them.

"Go on, then. Which one?"

Immediately, Miss Bellini's gloved forefinger taps the one on my right. "I think that one."

"You sure?" I ask her cheekily.

Miss Bellini spreads her hands.

I lift the cup, and the ball has gone.

She smiles, nods in approval. "Now the others."

I lift the second cup, and find nothing under it. And the third — and there's nothing there either. The ball has disappeared.

Miss Bellini claps delightedly. "Miranda! You've been practicing."

I shrug, smiling. "I've done my research. It's nothing to do with *magic*, or even sleight of hand. Just science, pure and simple." I flip the last cup up and trace my finger around the almost-invisible filigree of heat elements built into the smooth inner surface. "It cools really quickly. What's it made of?"

"A titanium alloy." Miss Bellini sounds very matter-of-fact. "Used by the US military in stealth bombers. Clever, isn't it?"

I nod. "And the ball — something that . . . sublimates quickly? Turns really easily from a solid into a gas?"

Miss Bellini nods. "A mutated allotrope of liquid nitrogen. One that's safe to handle. Under slight heat, it dissolves in seconds, leaving no trace — just colorless, odorless, non-toxic gas. A gas found in abundance in the atmosphere." Miss Bellini gives me a broad, satisfied grin. "You worked out most of it, though, Miranda. Congratulations."

I knew she hadn't spirited the ball away with sleight of hand. But what about a residue? Well, Miss Bellini herself taught us all about sublimation — turning from solid to gas — in Science just a week or so ago. She did it with iodine, but other things sublimate, too. So all that was left then was to ask where the heat for the process came from. I didn't know that for certain until a few minutes ago when I inspected the inner surface of the hemispherical cups a little more closely. Near-invisible, thread-thin heat elements, inlaid into the inner surface, and activated by pressing your fingers down on the top of the cup.

"You know," says Miss Bellini, "I often think about what Arthur C. Clarke said."

"The *2001* bloke?"

"Yes. He said that any sufficiently advanced technology is almost indistinguishable from magic. We need to keep open minds, Miranda, but always to be analytical. Rushing headlong at a problem with an emotional response doesn't always work."

I'll catch you if you fall.

"Sometimes it does," I say.

I can tell she knows what I mean. That sometimes, thinking isn't enough and you just have to go with what you feel is right.

"Come with me," says Miss Bellini. "There's one more thing I need to show you. Oh, and — you'll need a coat."

SEAVIEW HOTEL, BASEMENT: SATURDAY 12:37

The elevator is one of those old, creaky, wooden ones, even more dark and cramped than the one from the lobby. We descend in silence.

At last it clunks to a halt, and Miss Bellini opens it up manually, moving aside the double accordion doors. They make a deep, rattling, rumbling sound that echoes through the area where we have stopped so I get a sense of the space. As far as I can see, it's like some huge loading bay, lined with shelves.

I've been down to the storage basement before, Level Zero, to fetch boxes of printer paper and stuff like that — but I know straightaway that's not where we are. It feels wrong.

"Where are we?" I ask. There's a dusty, musty smell, and it's cold — an unearthly chill seeps from every surface and the air is wintry, like the sort you can almost bite when there is snow on the way.

I see now why she told me to bring my jacket. I zip it up, and button the collar across as well.

"Level Minus One," Miss Bellini says softly.

I look up at her. "I didn't know we had a Level Minus One."

I glance back at the column of buttons on the still-open elevator behind us. They stop at zero.

She gives me a quick smile. "We don't. Officially. They call it *plausible deniability*."

"What does that mean?"

"It means that if anyone comes sniffing around, nobody knows about it." Miss Bellini extends her left arm, and reaches out with her right hand to the gold watch on her left wrist.

There is a *click*, then a loud *CHUNG!* and a bank of strip lights suddenly turns on above us.

I blink.

A sequence of similar *CHUNG!* sounds repeats into the distance as more lights come on farther and farther away from us, slowly revealing a metal walkway about three feet or so off the ground. It's lined with banks of what look like filing cabinets. I can see other similar walkways disappearing off in the distance, at different levels.

"Welcome," says Miss Bellini, "to the Archive."

I swallow hard, look at the vast expanse before me. "This must go farther than underneath the Seaview Hotel."

"It does. These were old wartime bunkers. You'll need to know about this, for the future, now that you're sticking around. You are sticking around, I take it? Good. Come this way."

I notice she didn't wait for an answer to that question. I follow her along the metal walkway, our footsteps clanging and echoing, our shadows intense under the harsh white light.

Each of the filing cabinets, or lockers, or whatever they are, has a chunky, nine-figure keypad on the door instead of a normal lock.

"What's in these?" I ask.

"Impounded materials," says Miss Bellini. "The digital age is all very well, but some things just can't be reduced to pixels."

"Impounded?" I ask. "There's so much of it."

Miss Bellini smiles. "I've been busy. Ten years, more or less, before I came here and got this team together. The fruits of my work."

We climb a short bank of metal stairs and reach a circular, open area at the end of the banks of lockers where the lighting is dimmer and more purple.

Miss Bellini holds something up. "We have an addition to the collection," she says.

It's the yellow cylinder. It's been labeled with a bar code and stamped with a date.

"The Animus?" I say with a slight shiver.

Miss Bellini nods curtly. "What's left of it. Yes. Hold it." She throws it to me.

I jump as I catch the cylinder.

I stare at the matte yellow surface, holding it carefully with my fingertips as Miss Bellini twists her watch dial again.

There is another *CHUNG!* sound, and this time, a dozen or so blue pillars of light stab downward, making pools of radiance on the floor in front of us in a semicircular shape. Inside each one is what looks like a smoked-glass pillar, mounted with a small control panel.

Miss Bellini goes to the nearest one, punches a code in, and the pillar pulls upward to head-height. She snaps her fingers, and I give her the yellow cylinder.

"Maximum containment," says Miss Bellini by way of explanation. "Only for the most dangerous items."

She throws the cylinder into the column of light. To my astonishment, it doesn't drop. It just hangs there in midair.

"How do you do that?"

"Magnetic fields, mainly. You know about Faraday?"

I nod. Science, after all, is one class where I do pay attention.

"There you are, then." Miss Bellini steps back, and the glass pillar descends. She punches a code into the panel again. "That's contained."

I'm still staring at the small cylinder, floating there, cushioned by nothingness.

I think about the Animus. All the centuries she lived, and the miles she traveled, the things she saw. Always finding sources of heat, and light, and energy. Absorbing, exhaling. Absorbing, exhaling. Caught forever in the cycle of the fire that had saved her from the Plague, but condemned her to eternal life.

All those personalities. All those lives. All those experiences and loves and . . .

"Miss Bellini," I ask, "I didn't *kill* her, did I?"

Miss Bellini sighs and puts an arm gently around my shoulders. "Child," she says, "she was not *alive*, not in the sense you and I understand. Her normal human form would have survived for, what, fifty years at most as a woman in the Middle Ages? She should not have *been* in this place, in this time. We have set things right."

I look up, smile. "Of course," I say. "Of course we have."

"And, in a way," says Miss Bellini, "she helped us."

"She did?"

Miss Bellini nods, gazing into the dark vaults. "Creatures like the Animus, you see, may not actually be the enemy we face. They are merely . . . manifestations of its effects, if you like. If the enemy is a fire, then they are the flickering shadows upon the wall, the sparks borne upon the breeze and swirling like fireflies into the night."

"That's very poetic, Miss Bellini. I wish I knew what it meant."

"You will." Miss Bellini twists her watch again and the pillar lights go out. "Come on," she says. "I need to talk to you with the others."

She turns and heads off back down the walkway, toward the elevator, heels clanging on the metal.

I look over my shoulder one last time, into the blackness of the Archive behind me.

And then I plunge my hands into the pockets of my jacket, and follow Miss Bellini to the elevator.

* * *

Miss Bellini looks at each of us in turn, keeping her hands clasped neatly together, as she often does when she has something important to convey. "You all did very well the other day," she says. "I'm pleased with you."

I think about the networks my mother mentioned. I wonder if anyone else has heard and is pleased with us.

We look at one another, smiling proudly. We can't help it.

"Now, the thing is," says Miss Bellini, "there's going to have to be a little . . . restructuring around here. I want to ask Miranda to join us full-time."

"Well," says Cal, "as close to full-time as any of us can be. With schoolwork and all that."

"Indeed," says Miss Bellini. "But nobody here seems to have a problem with that. . . . You know we need someone like you, Miranda, not just for your gifts. . . . We need someone who's got a little edge. Someone not just with the courage to make decisions, but the daring to do things a little differently. Like you said before — it's not necessarily just about thinking."

I feel nervous of the group. Do I really belong here? Over the last few days I have been wondering what would happen, now that this is all over. Because I know they have been investigating many strange occurrences in Firecroft Bay, and I know Ollie, for one, needs a question answered. . . . Perhaps the others do, too. And then there are those horses.

I don't like unanswered questions. But that's what life has.

"I don't know if I'm ready to do that," I say, but as I hear myself say it I am not convinced.

"You're already part of the group, Miranda May." Miss Bellini leans forward, her mouth wearing just the hint — just the shadow — of a smile. Her eyes are bright and black behind her glasses. "I couldn't see what was under my nose, guys. That scares me. Does it scare you? It should. It's made me think a few things through."

"I'm still not sure about all this," I say. "I'm only twelve!"

"Thirteen next week, I gather." She raises her eyebrows.

Blimey. With everything else that's been going on, I'd completely forgotten about my own birthday.

Ohhh . . . bowling. *That's* what my mum was talking about. My birthday party.

She was asking me if I still wanted to go bowling for my birthday, and I acted like a total dumbo. I feel like smacking my forehead with my open palm, like they do in sitcoms.

"So?" says Miss Bellini. "What's it to be, Miranda? Yes or no?"

"I won't let you down, Miss Bellini," I say.

She nods. "I know," she says. "You are special, Miranda, and we need you as much as you need us."

She holds my gaze for a second longer before turning and going back up into the Pod.

Nervously, I turn and look up at Josh. His eyes are half hidden by his hair, and his expression is giving nothing away.

Eventually, he says, "Welcome to the team, then. *Special* Girl." There's a bit of an edge to that.

I shrug. "I feel . . . a bit awkward." I smile at the others. "I'm sure I'll get used to it, guys."

There's a moment's pause.

"You will," Cal says softly.

Lyssa and Ollie smile.

"It'll be good to have you around," says Ollie, nodding affably.

"Girls outnumber the boys now," Lyssa points out with a cheeky grin.

I smile. "Thanks. And I mean it. I won't let you down."

Oh, and they know I'll be watching them, too. After all, they weren't averse to using me when it was necessary.

Josh strolls over to the pool table. It's still my turn, but I don't say anything. In one smooth movement he lines up the shot, leans in, clicks the cue, and sends the white cannoning into the black. It powers across the table and slams into the far pocket.

He saunters back over, hands the cue back to me.

"Well," he says, and half smiles. "I think you'll fit in just fine."

I smile back at him, and I see something in his mischievous eyes behind that floppy hair. What is it? Trust, affection, friendliness? Or something more? For the moment, I can't tell.

It looks like we are back in business.

Whatever happens.

* * *

My name is Miranda Keira May. I am thirteen years old, and I'm an ordinary girl, living an extraordinary life.

In this place at the edge of the world, my friends and I see things we're not supposed to see. And we know things we're not meant to know. About ghosts and demons and conspiracies. In this place where the land meets the sea, where fantasy meets reality, where dreams meet wakefulness. This town of history, of myth, of secrets. Of life at the borders of what you call reality. The stuff the authorities haven't got time for, the tales your parents tell you are just stories.

There's a darkness falling across the land, and we can see it.

And we're being trained by our mentor, Miss Bellini, to face it.

We're just a bunch of kids — the perfect front for the perfect undercover organization. We investigate the weird, understand the strange, think the unthinkable, restore the balance of the world.

You'd better believe in us. We're here to save you.

Nobody else will.

You see, this is how it is, this is the way the world turns. This is what I've learned.

That darkness at the edge of town, the whisper in the grass like a passing ghost, the shapes in the corner of your room, the shadows outside in the streetlights, and the things that come in your dreams . . .

They all tell us something.

There is more to this existence than I ever imagined. There is more to this life than I could ever have known.

These things come from another place. And they're all real. As real as streets, and houses, and cars. As real as your family, and your friends. As real as fear, and as real as pain and regret.

And as real as love.

ACKNOWLEDGMENTS

I would like to thank Arts Council England for providing a generous grant, which contributed greatly to my being able to complete the earliest draft of this novel, and also my friend, the poet Rob Hindle, for giving me the inspiration to apply in the first place.

Thanks to the Chicken House team for their enthusiasm, and helpful and constructive input at all times, and to Caroline Montgomery for being such a hardworking and diligent agent.

As ever, my love to Rachel, Elinor, and Samuel for being my supportive and long-suffering family.

My dad, Brian Edwin Blythe, died a few months before the final draft of this book was completed. It is dedicated to his memory, and the memory of the many times he took me to the library and started a lifelong love of reading.